Dangerous Liasons

"I want to go, too."

Slocum shook his head. "I can't let you. Too dangerous. You know no one. No. If it was your village, I'd say okay. But you don't know who you can trust in there."

"I am not a child."

He took her threatening fist into his own, and slipped away with her in a waltz. The crowd was growing and the revelry grew louder.

"You're not even thinking about it, are you?" she demanded.

"I'm thinking I don't want to see you dead. This man's a rabid killer."

She hugged him. "I want to help you, understand?"

He moved her in small circles through the crowd. "Too damn dangerous."

"We'll see what's dangerous when we get into bed tonight."

Slocum pulled her closer, so he could feel her body against his. There would sure be a fight—but he knew when she made her mind up, Hell couldn't stop her.

JAKE LOGAN

SLOCUM
AND THE
BANDIT DURANGO

JOVE BOOKS, NEW YORK

THE BERKLEY PUBLISHING GROUP
Published by the Penguin Group
Penguin Group (USA) Inc.
375 Hudson Street, New York, New York 10014, USA
Penguin Group (Canada), 90 Eglinton Avenue East, Suite 700, Toronto, Ontario M4P 2Y3, Canada
(a division of Pearson Penguin Canada Inc.)
Penguin Books Ltd., 80 Strand, London WC2R 0RL, England
Penguin Group Ireland, 25 St. Stephen's Green, Dublin 2, Ireland (a division of Penguin Books Ltd.)
Penguin Group (Australia), 250 Camberwell Road, Camberwell, Victoria 3124, Australia
(a division of Pearson Australia Group Pty. Ltd.)
Penguin Books India Pvt. Ltd., 11 Community Centre, Panchsheel Park, New Delhi—110 017, India
Penguin Group (NZ), 67 Apollo Drive, Rosedale, North Shore 0632, New Zealand
(a division of Pearson New Zealand Ltd.)
Penguin Books (South Africa) (Pty.) Ltd., 24 Sturdee Avenue, Rosebank, Johannesburg 2196,
South Africa

Penguin Books Ltd., Registered Offices: 80 Strand, London WC2R 0RL, England

This is a work of fiction. Names, characters, places, and incidents either are the product of the author's imagination or are used fictitiously, and any resemblance to actual persons, living or dead, business establishments, events, or locales is entirely coincidental.

SLOCUM AND THE BANDIT DURANGO

A Jove Book / published by arrangement with the author

PRINTING HISTORY
Jove edition / December 2008

ISBN: 978-0-515-14551-9

JOVE®
Jove Books are published by The Berkley Publishing Group,
a division of Penguin Group (USA) Inc.
375 Hudson Street, New York, New York 10014.
JOVE® is a registered trademark of Penguin Group (USA) Inc.
The "J" design is a trademark belonging to Penguin Group (USA) Inc.

PRINTED IN THE UNITED STATES OF AMERICA

10 9 8 7 6 5 4 3 2 1

Prologue

With her thick arms folded over her large bust, Madame Mustache stood in his way. Dressed in a low-cut, ruby red velvet dress, she planted her lace-up black shoes on the polished hardwood floor, blocking him from getting past her. Her upper lip was covered with coarse black hair. That's why he called her Madame Mustache instead of Cheery O'Leary, her real name.

"I must talk to Señor Benton," Enrique Jimenez said, feeling overpowered by this six-foot-tall woman with the long wavy dark hair, standing in front of him with her breathtaking perfume.

"Señor Benton is busy right now."

"But I have ridden many miles to find him. Many people's lives depend on me getting to talk to him."

"Your skinny ass ain't worth getting blown off. He don't like being disturbed when he's busy."

"I came from many miles to seek him."

"Go upstairs and get blown to smithereens. I ain't gonna be responsible. He's in Room Three."

"*Gracias, gracias,*" he said, edging around her and swallowing hard. Such a huge woman—to be in bed with her would be like trying to make love to all the Sierra Madres.

He put on his straw sombrero, and his gritty sandals took the polished wooden steps two at a time. This palatial whore-house with the big chandelier hanging from its high ceiling made him feel inadequate.

He stopped before Room Three and listened with his ear to the door.

"Get your butt up more."

"I am, I am," a woman's voice complained.

He grunted like a pig. "There. Now I'm getting deep enough."

"That hurts," she whined.

"It won't for long—"

Enrique could wait no more. He began knocking.

"Who in the hell's out there?"

"Enrique, Enrique Jimenez, Señor."

"Get the hell out of here. Can't you tell—" He grunted again. "Come back later."

"The outlaw Durango has taken over our village. He and his men are raping our women."

"Ain't no damn worry of mine—ah, shitfire—just quit. I'll go send him away."

"But you have no pants on," the woman said, aghast.

"Fuck the pants," he said to her, and then unbolted the door. He stood in the partially open doorway with his half-expired erection sticking out from under his shirttail. "You live at Antonio?"

"Sí, Señor. Durango is back in my village. They are rap-ing little girls even."

Benton was a short man. His salt and pepper handlebar mustache drooped on the ends and his blue eyes looked like the sky, but they missed no detail. "Ride up to Mesilla and find Slocum. If he thinks we should go help you, I'll go along." He started to close the door.

"*Gracias, señor. Gracias, señor.* Do you know where I can find Señor Slocum in Mesilla?"

"Hell, try the whorehouses first, then any good-looking widow women. You'll find him."

"I will, Señor."

"Now get the damn hell out of here!" Benton slammed the door and shouted at the whore, "Get your ass back in bed. I ain't done with you yet."

Encouraged by the man's words—*If he thinks we should go help you, I'll go along*—Jimenez came down the stairs two at a time, and almost collided with with Madame Mustache.

"What did he tell you?"

"That he would help my people. I must go find Señor Slocum in Mesilla."

She raised one of her sleepy eyelids toward the head of the stairs. "What can that old man up there do for you against these outlaws you speak about?"

Enrique turned an ear to the cries of the woman in Room Three. He smiled. "There is a saying in my land that snow on the mountain does not mean the fire went out."

The moaning from Room Three grew even louder, and then all at once the woman went silent.

"Sumbitch. Why, she's fainted," Madame Mustache said. She put a large hand with many rings on her fingers atop the curled end of the railing, halting Enrique's exit. She looked at the upstairs in disbelief and then shook her head. "I'll be gawdamned. That old son of a bitch made her faint. I've heard it all now."

"Excuse me. I must ride to Mesilla."

She turned enough to let him slip by and he was past her in a flash. Mesilla was many miles up the road from El Paso. He had no time to waste.

Before he reached the cut-glass front door, she shouted, "Don't slam it."

"I won't, Señora."

* * *

It was before dawn the next day when Enrique ran inside the ornate El Morocco Bar in Mesilla. An old man sat on a bar stool as if he'd been there all night. Bent over with age, he cast a look down the bar at Enrique. "What in the hell do you want?"

"I am looking for Señor Slocum."

The old man chuckled. "He ain't no Señor." He waved Enrique closer, and did it again when Enrique did not move. "Get down here. I'm a damn good friend of Slocum."

"I must talk to him right away."

"Have a stool." He patted one beside him.

Enrique felt suspicious of this craggy-faced hombre. What did he want from him?

"You want Slocum, you've got to listen to me," the old man said, slurring his words a little from drinking.

"Do you know where he is at?" Enrique asked.

"Hell, yes, I know right where he's at, boy. Now what do you expect from him?"

"There is an outlaw named Durango who is holding the people in my village hostage in Mexico. I need him and Señor Benton to help me drive them away."

The old man leaned back on his stool and looked Enrique over. "Ha, a hatch-ass like you would need more than them two to help you."

"I know of no one else I can ask for help, Señor."

"Well—" The old man finished his drink in one gulp and slammed the glass down. "By God, boy, we'll go find the man hisself."

Gracias, señor.

Enrique started for the door, hoping the old man was right behind him. When he looked back for him, the old man was busy counting coins from a handful of change to pay his bar bill. Then he thanked the bartender and started in a stoop-shouldered walk toward the front door. Dressed in the clothing of gringos, he wore a snap-brim straw hat with a wide cloth band on which pictures of naked girls were hand-painted. His feet were in sandals.

Outside, Enrique was already in the saddle of his weary bay mustang, Pedro. He'd ridden the tough wiry bronc hard for many days. The old man went around the side of the building, and soon came back leading a medium-sized white mule.

"Whoa. Whoa, Blanco," he growled at the animal, jerking on the bridle until Blanco stood still. "Damned old mule anyway."

He used his free hand to pull his left leg up and inserted his foot in the iron stirrup, and then, talking aloud to the animal the entire time, he sat on the McClellan saddle. When the reins were gathered, he wheeled the mule around and set out in a dead run down the street. To catch up with this crazy old man, Enrique had to spur Pedro after him.

"My name is Dyke," the man shouted at him as they loped their horses in the darkness through the flat farmland. "Dyke Von Schultz."

"*Sí, señor.*" Enrique wondered how far they had to go.

"Damnit, call me Dyke, boy."

"*Sí*—Dyke."

"Now tell me about this bastard Durango."

"He was once a small bandit. He robbed some lone men on the road. Then he tried to be a big bandit. One day, he brought his gang to the cantina in Antonio. But Señor Slocum and Señor Benton were there having what you call a celebration.

"Mother of God, I swear they killed three of the gang. Busted up some more, and then they took Durango and those still alive to the *federales* and had them thrown in prison for life."

"How in the hell did they get out?"

"Oh, Señor, someone probably sent a *político* some money and Durango was pardoned. There is much corruption in my country."

"I know that. I know that."

"How far is it to Señor Slocum? My horse Pedro, he is getting *mucho* tired."

"Why, hell, we'll slow down then. Whoa."

They rode down a sandy wash and soon skirted the Rio Grande. Cottonwood trees rustled and birds began to sing in the predawn.

Dyke turned his mule up a driveway. The rising sun shone on the red tile roof of the two-story house. This was a great house that in the sunrise looked like the finest hacienda that Enrique had ever seen.

"This the señor's ranch?" Enrique asked Dyke.

The old man shook his head.

"Your ranch?"

"No, this belongs to Adriana Morales Garcia."

"Who is she?"

Dyke grinned at him. "A rich bitch that really likes Slocum." Then he broke out laughing and slapped his knee. "By God, I mean a real rich one, too."

Enrique nodded. He hoped he could talk Slocum into leaving this *grande casa* and going back to Mexico with him and Benton. He looked at the brightening sky and crossed himself. "Mother of God, help me . . ."

They reined up before the large house. Dyke kicked out of the stirrups and scrambled off his mule. Enrique stopped the tired Pedro and stepped down. His leg muscles were as tight as a bowstring. It was unusual for him to be at the front entrance of such a place as this. If he had not come with this snow-whiskered old man, he would never have been there when Dyke knocked on the tall double doors.

"Señor Von Schultz," a buxom Hispanic woman shouted, and hugged him.

She had such big breasts that Enrique wondered, as short as he was, if she'd smother him to death in between them with such a hug.

"Reya, this here is Señor Jimenez. He's come all the way from Mexico to see his amigo Slocum."

To Enrique's relief, she curtsied. "Señor Slocum is in the kitchen. I will get him at once."

Dyke had taken off the naked lady hat, and was tapping it against his leg as they walked into the tile-floored front room. Enrique held his filthy straw sombrero. The tall arches above him led to a high-ceilinged room beyond. He could hear a fountain in that room. Maybe it had a statue of a boy peeing. He saw one once in Quaymas. That was the farthest he had ever been from his mountain valley until now.

"Enrique, mi amigo," Slocum shouted, and his voice reverberated in the great room as he crossed it. "Dyke, where did you find him?"

Enrique felt much better when the big man recognized him and hugged him.

"He came in the El Morocco looking for you," Dyke said.

Slocum led them across the great room and past a long black walnut table that had high-back chairs covered with red velvet like those kings sat on. The whole place awed Enrique. Then they entered the kitchen, which smelled of cinnamon, and he saw some coffee-colored faces look up and smile.

"What brings you here, Enrique?" Slocum asked.

"Coffee?" a lovely young girl said with cups in one hand and a pot in the other.

"Hell, no, I never drink that sh—stuff," Dyke said, as if he was offended that she'd even offered him some. "Bring me some scotch."

"Will you have some coffee?" she asked Enrique. She looked hurt by the old man's gruffness.

"Sí, muchas gracias," Enrique said. He couldn't take his eyes off her. She had a perfect figure, with slender willowy hips and budding high breasts. Swallowing became hard for him.

"I am sorry, Señor Slocum," he said. "I have been very busy trying to find you and Señor Benton. I found him yesterday in El Paso—" He looked around to see if any of the women were close enough to hear him. "He was in a house and he said if you would go—"

"Here is your scotch," Reya said, delivering the bottle and a glass to Dyke.

The old man set them down on the counter. "Now ain't you lovely." Then he did a dance with her around the kitchen. "By damn, a girl of my own heart."

"Señor, he said if you would go, he would go, too," said Enrique.

Then Dyke kissed Reya real hard and bent her over backward. His actions drew cheers and whistles from the kitchen crew. He pulled her up and spun her around to their applause.

Enrique tried again. "He said if you would help us, he would, too."

Slocum nodded, and they all turned as a dark-haired woman swept into the room in a fancy blue dress. No one spoke until Dyke reached over, splashed some scotch in a glass, and raised a toast.

"To the grand lady of the casa. To Adriana. Everyone get their glasses. This is a toast to her."

For a moment, no one spoke. Then, out of nowhere, the pretty girl put half a glass of red wine in Enrique's hand, then ducked away. Mechanically, he raised the glass in salute—grateful for her quick actions on his behalf.

"To the loveliest lady on the Rio Grande north to south," Dyke said. "Clear to the gulf."

She smiled, as if a little embarrassed, and then turned to Enrique. "You have heard my name. What is yours?"

"Enrique Jimenez. He lives in a beautiful valley in the Madres," Slocum said when Enrique stood there tongue-tied.

"Nice to meet you, Señora," he finally managed.

"My, we have started a party already. Have fun, Señor Jimenez. You may all continue. I must see about some paperwork. Slocum, you must entertain him." She hugged Slocum's waist possessively, bumping her hip to his leg.

He put his arm around her shoulder and kissed her. Then, tapping her lightly on the nose with a forefinger, he said. "We will try not to be too loud."

She smiled at his words, and everyone relaxed. "And you old coyote," she said to Dyke, "have you broken any more young widows' hearts lately?"

When she offered her cheek, he kissed it formally. "No, but I am willing to do it with you," he replied.

She looked amused at his words and shook her head at him. Then, with a wave, she left the kitchen.

"You haven't said anything, Señor," Enrique said to Slocum.

Slocum nodded.

1

He studied the mug of pulque, the homemade beer he loved. The guitar and trumpet music made the lone woman whirl around the floor with her arms over her head moving like willow limbs. Her shapely hips were revolving for him, the long breasts under the blouse were shaking to arouse him. Lupe Serra was perhaps thirty. She was the mayor's wife and ripe for plowing by him.

A chuckle rose in his throat as he clapped to her dancing. When he had summoned her husband to the cantina, that coward had pissed in his pants. Now he was somewhere in the hills above the village, shaking in fear, having left his lovely wife's ass for Durango to use. Ah, this valley was his. How could these sniveling peons ever rise up and take his command away?

That fucking gringo Slocum was running from the law, Durango heard, and that Texas lawman had lost his badge and spent all his time in border whorehouses. Those two had spoiled his plans the last time when he had come to take over this valley. But neither of them would be able to come back here again and interfere with his control of Antonio and the valley. He'd never forgive those two for the years he'd spent in prison because of them. He'd had to pay that stinking Ramirez to screw his wife when she came on conjugal visits. She had flabby breasts and a doughy belly from having so many babies. And she stank like she never wiped her ass, besides being ugly as a monkey.

When the music was over, the dizzy Lupe staggered off the floor in her high heels toward him. He caught her in his arms in time to stop her from falling. She threw her hair back and presented her face for him to kiss. His lips closed on hers and her hot tongue sought his teeth. What a bitch in heat.

Her hand groped at his crotch, and she raised up to whisper in his ear, "Take me. Now!"

He swooped her up in his arms to a cheer from his men in the cantina. Her leg kicked like a stern-wheel paddle boat and she shrieked in his ear. His men applauded him as he went into the side room he used as his office and bedroom.

He put her on the bed and began to undress. She fumbled with the small buttons down the front of her dress, spilling out the long breasts. He swung off his gun belt. She shrugged off the dress and flung it on the chair that he hung his holster on. She tore the slip off over her head, and was hugging him and rubbing her pubic mound against his leg as he shed his boots, then his pants.

Naked from the waist down, he gripped his half-full cock at the base and nosed it in between her legs. She reached back and caught her foot so she could spread her crotch open, and he jammed it in her with both of them standing. Forced to cling to him with her free hand, she moaned as he jabbed it to her. Holding the cheeks of her butt in both hands, he pumped it in deeper and harder.

"Oh, oh," she cried. "Get on the bed, I have a cramp."

They parted for a second as she fell on her back in the bed. With her knees flat on the bed, he stuffed his aching dick back inside her. She raised her butt up to accept him. Once past the ring, he felt the viselike hold she used on him. Soon, they were both off in some foreign land of swirling fog, their efforts harder and harder. His butt became an angry pile driver that went deeper and deeper, until he felt a hot Indian lance in his rectum and exploded.

She tossed her head on the pillow as if shaken by the event. "It was so good."

"Yes," he said on his knees over her, busy fondling her breasts.

Her sleepy grin told him she didn't care. In fact, she enjoyed attention in any form, especially from his big dick. He reached down and began to play with her pussy. In seconds, her large clit grew stiff. He took it between his fingers and began to jack it off. It cut off her hard breathing with a gasp. She raised her butt clear of the bed, arched her back in a bow, and hunched at his swift milking of her erection, tossing her head in total abandonment.

Her mouth open wide, she let out a short, sharp cry and collapsed in a faint on her side. He pulled her up on her knees. She was moaning and mumbling like a drunk as he steadied her with one hand and reached underneath her with the other to spread her legs apart and smear the gooey juices over her crack. Then he probed her butt with a slick finger, and she moaned even more. With a free hand, she tried to wave him away, but he moved between her legs and with the head of his dick covered in her slime, he pulled his fingers out.

Before she could utter a word, he cut off any scream with his right hand closed over her mouth. Then he drove his hard-on into her rectum. It was tight and she squirmed, but he was enjoying it too much not to go for it. His short strokes went deeper and deeper, until he came hard enough that his balls cramped and she collapsed.

He raised up and smiled as she held her backside and softly cried, "Don't you know that hurt me?"

Leaning over, he kissed her on her wet cheek. "It always does the first time."

He dressed and went back in the cantina to drink pulque

with his *compañeros*. After a good session of pussy, he liked
to go back to the company of men and let them know he was
a cockerel. The music played loud and many men shuffle-
danced with their women.

His army of convicts had all been pardoned because
of his generosity. They would be loyal to him or go back behind bars again—many for the rest of their lives. All he had
to do was snap his fingers and back they went to the cala-
boose forever. He told them they could choose a wife in the
valley, but they had to act as husbands. To that they agreed,
and many had sent the women's men away. A few women
were made widows, but most men, like the mayor, quickly
ran away.

They were simple farmers, with no guns, no weapons,
and no fight in them. As long as sons of bitches like Slocum
did not come around, Durango would rule.

Who was that girl dancing? He leaned over to Mucho.
"Who is she? That short one who is dancing by herself."

"Marisel is her name." He shook his head. "I don't
know her last name."

"Does she have a man?" He held his mug up and in-
haled the sour fermented smell he loved.

"I don't know, Captain. I will get her for you."

"No, but tell everyone to stay away from her. I want her
when I get ready."

"*Sí*, Captain. I will tell them to keep their dirty dicks out
of her. She is my captain's own."

"Good, pass the word."

"You through with the mayor's wife?"

"Not yet." He made a face, then grinned. "But a captain
can plow many fields, no?"

"Ah, yes, many fields."

Why was such a small-assed girl so intriguing to him?
Never mind. Her eyes sparkled like polished coal, and the
set to her mouth made him hungry to kiss her. Women,
women, he loved many of them.

"Refill my cup," he said to the bartender, José.

"*Sí, señor.* The corn is coming this week. I have no money to pay for it," José said, busy scrubbing the bar before him with a cloth.

"How much will that bill be?"

"Thirty-forty pesos."

"In the morning see me. I will give you the money to pay for the corn. We have to have pulque."

"The beer and the wine comes later this week."

"How much will it be?"

"Oh, a hundred pesos."

"It is expensive being a mayor, huh?"

"Oh, *sí, señor.* But I do not charge your men."

He held up his hand to silence the man. "I will pay for it."

"*Gracias, señor.*" José refilled his mug until the foam ran over the lip.

"*Bueno, mi amigo.*" Durango toasted him with the mug.

Later, when he went back to the room, he found his bed was empty and Lupe gone. Ah, she must have gone home. He undressed and lay in the bed. After she slept on the floor in that jacal a few nights, she would be back begging for his dick. He jacked off until he came, but it never satisfied him.

He wondered about the small dancer. Where did she sleep? Then he shut his eyes until early morning when a rooster crowed. Barefoot, he stepped outside, careful to not step on any goat-head thorns with his tender soles. He was pissing a stream out into the soft predawn light when he heard his second in command, Tomas, calling for him.

"Captain, captain—oh, you are awake. I was afraid of waking your woman, too."

"She went home last night. What is wrong?"

"They killed one of our men last night."

"How? Who was the man they killed?"

"Obregon was his name. They caved his head in with a club, we think."

"He the one had a bad scar on his right cheek?"

"Yes."

"We can't allow this to happen. His woman's husband probably came back and killed him. Where is he?"

Tomas shook his head. "She said he is gone."

"I will get dressed. We must handle this at once. Have them bring my stallion Eagle around and I will ride up there. We must make them believe we can handle such things. How many children?"

"Three, I think."

"Have them and her there."

"Yes, Captain."

He went inside and quickly dressed. Outside, as he pulled on his boots, he could hear the arrival of his gray stallion. Such a grand animal under a fancy silver-mounted saddle and bridle—mounted on him, he looked like both mayor and judge.

Eagle splashed across the knee-deep river and up under the cottonwoods past the small plots and casas of the residents. Durango came to where some of his men stood in the road. A boy took his reins. In front of the casa, on the ground, was his man's body lying facedown. The back of his head was caved in.

No doubt he'd been murdered. Durango looked at the woman who stood there staring at the ground. He walked over and with a handful of hair, lifted her head to look her in the eye.

"Who killed *mi amigo*?"

"I don't know."

"You know. Your man came home and killed him. Didn't he?"

"No, no. I don't know."

"If I strip you naked, will that improve your memory?"

"Madre de Dios, have mercy. I found him—" She was on her knees begging.

"Strip her clothes off and hold her up. She's lost her memory. Naked, it will come back to her."

"Oh, no, oh, no," she moaned as they carried out his orders. Then two soldiers held her up between them, and he stepped in, grabbed a handful of hair, and jerked her head up.

"Your husband killed my man—didn't he?"

"Yes, yes, let me dress, oh, please—"

"Where is he?"

Hysterically, she screamed, "I don't know."

"Bring that boy over here," he said to the man standing behind him. Then he turned back to her. "For your boy's life, will you tell me where he is at?"

"Oh, no—"

Durango drew the side of his own hand over his own throat. The soldier cut the boy's throat before he could utter a word, and then threw him aside.

"No! no," she cried.

"The girl is next." He pointed to the young girl, who was maybe five. "Where is he?"

"I—don't—know—" Then she went into hysterics as he told Tomas to execute the girl.

"There is one left—" He again jerked the woman's head up. "She will die, too." The woman babbled incoherently.

"Last chance. Where is he?"

She shook her head and sagged between the two soldiers. "Don't, don't, not her."

"Where is he?"

"I don't know!"

He gave the order to Tomas. The small one's throat was sliced open and she was tossed on the pile of the dead like rubbish. Several of the men cleared their throats. A few went behind the jacal to vomit.

"You want to live, tell me where he is hiding."

She was ranting and raving—there was no repentance in her fiery eyes. She'd lured his man in and then her husband, who'd snuck home like a coyote, had killed him, probably while he was screwing her.

•

Durango reached over, jerked her up on her toes with a handful of hair in his left hand, and made one wide sweep of his razor-sharp bowie knife, severing her arteries and her vocal cords to her spinal column. Then the soldiers let go and he shoved her away. On the ground, her short bare legs churned up dust in her involuntary kicking.

"Next time, more of you can do the executing." He left the yard wiping the blade clean on his leather pants. Mounted, he rode his prancing stallion back to the cantina.

Who was that dancer? Maybe Lupe was back. If not, he'd have the bar maid Nalda give him a blow job.

2

In the predawn, Slocum, seated in the flower garden, drank rich hot coffee from a mug. He heard footsteps on the flagstones as the morning doves and quail began to sing, and turned to see who was invading his private moments.

"More coffee?" Adriana asked, holding a pitcher like a servant girl.

"Sure. What has you up so early?"

"You." She stood before him in a Turkish robe and poured his cup full, then poured some for herself in another cup.

"Why me?"

Then she swept the robe under her as she took a chair opposite him. "You never said last night what you would do about that boy's request."

Pained by what he must tell her, he looked off at the brightening sky. "I guess I better go see what I can do. Those are lovely people who live in that valley."

"You leave anyone there?"

"No. I met Buck Benton in Mexico. He was sheriff over by Fredericksburg in Gillespie County, Texas. Three men robbed and murdered a rich rancher in his district. He set out to capture them. Two of them, Morris and Calhoun, he

19

captured around Ruidoso and sent them back with a deputy. The third man, named Dane, ran into Mexico. I met Buck down there and he never asked me a question about my past. He understood I knew the Madres and hired me as his guide.

"We found this Marty Dane working at a mine. Right away, when we told him who we were, he went for his gun. We buried him down there and went down to Antonio to put on a small fandango just as this two-bit bandit showed up with his gang to take over things.

"In about three minutes, that many of his gang were on the floor, and we hauled him and some more we thought might live to the *federales,* and they gave them life prison sentences."

He sipped some coffee and then leaned back. "When Buck finally got home, they'd elected a new sheriff thinking he was dead, but he brought about half that rancher's money back and got reelected."

Slocum smiled in amusement. "I guess he'd still be sheriff down there, but some high-powered state senator come home early from Austin and found him in bed with his wife."

She shook her head as if in disbelief. "And you're dead set on doing this?"

"Yes, the people in the valley don't have anyone else to turn to."

"Why it's any of your concern I can't imagine. You will need a pack train. There are no roads, right?"

"Barely trails. But you—"

She held up her palm to silence him. "What will you need for this crusade?"

"I'm not begging."

"I want to help these godforsaken people, too, since you're involved. Make me a list so I can fill it." She rose and picked up the pitcher. "Don't be skimpy. I have several mules coming this morning for your inspection. Will that be enough?"

"More than I deserve."

"That is your opinion." And she left him.

He stretched out his legs. A couple of hard days in the saddle might kill him. His empty cup in hand, he went inside the kitchen where the girls were working under Reya.

Seated on a stool, Enrique looked as anxious as he had the night before, despite his night spent in the bed of the lovely kitchen girl Manuela. He appeared bursting to ask Slocum if he was going to help his people, so Slocum beat him to the draw.

"The señora has some mules coming this morning," said Slocum. "Make sure they're sound enough to pack our things to the mountains. Then you go get Buck and meet us in Deming in four days."

"*Sí, señor.*"

"Did I hear someone mention some godforsaken town in the wilds?" Dyke asked in a roaring voice, coming in the kitchen. "Make a reservation for me. I'm going along."

Reya set out the bottle of scotch and glass for him on the long table, while the girls stopped their food preparation to make room for him.

"Dyke, why are you going along?" Slocum asked.

The older man held the glass of liquor up to the light overhead. "Good stuff. See, you can tell there aren't any sticks or stones in it." He made the girls giggle.

"Dyke, why in the hell are you going along?"

"For the news story. I'm a reporter for the *New York Chronicle*. My family owns that newspaper. Why, just last week I reported on the one-hundred-head burro race around the Mesilla square." He took a sip of the whiskey and nodded in satisfaction. "Where was I? Oh, yes, and when the race was over I was well on my way to a good evening and I couldn't find the winner's name, so I made Juan Rendosa the winner. But when I told that ungrateful swine I'd listed him as the winner to the entire world in my story that went to newspapers all over the globe, he said he came in fifth."

Slocum gave up. "We aren't drinking liquor on this trip."

Blinking in disbelief, Dyke looked over at him. "Fine. I'm still going along."

"Fix them some breakfast," Reya said to her helpers. "Or we won't ever get rid of them."

"Did I ever tell you I once worked as a chef?" Dyke said to her.

"How many people died from eating it?"

"It was in Paris—"

"Then get over here and help me make a supply list, Chef Dyke," Slocum said.

Everyone laughed as he joined Slocum.

Dyke pointed to the paper. "A hundred pounds of frijoles."

"I've got that."

"Baking powder, a hundred pounds of flour, fifty pounds of sugar, a couple of large tins of raisins and dried apples—oh, yes, add cinnamon, salt, pepper. Got lard down yet?"

"I'm adding it. Beef jerky." Slocum looked at his list.

"Salt pork, airtight tomatoes, and peaches. Need a couple Dutch ovens, skillets, coffeepot, some knives, aprons, towels, tin plates, utensils, and tin cups. Matches, a couple boxes of them. And some chili peppers."

"What do you know about blasting?"

Dyke nodded. "I know lots. We going mining?"

Slocum shook his head. "Not this time, but a stick of blasting powder thrown in a room can clear it out fast."

"It will. I've even tied them on arrows and fired them." Dyke drew back an imaginary bowstring and released it.

"Say four boxes of blasting sticks, caps, and lots of fuse cord?"

"Yes. One good mule can pack that and we'll keep him at the back of the string."

"Especially when the shooting starts."

"Come on, you hombres. Breakfast in the dining hall." Reya herded them into the great room to clear her kitchen.

Slocum sat back and sipped his coffee, considering his list. He added some .44/40 ammo.

Adriana came by and hugged his shoulder, looking over what he'd written down. "I hope I can afford all this. I suppose you should add some bandages, disinfectant, some needles and thread, tweezers, and laudanum." She looked at Slocum and Dyke.

"Good idea," Dyke said.

"I'll just buy a general store and send it up there," she said. Then she laughed, whipping her hair back over her shoulders. "May I join you?"

"Oh, yes, ma'am," Enrique said, shoving his chair back on the tile and standing up for her.

"Be seated, Enrique, I just wanted to hear them grumble about me joining them."

Slocum shook his head. "Have a seat, fair lady." He patted the one next to him and she accepted it.

When Dyke had rolled his eggs, peppers, red salsa, and ham in a tortilla, he finally pointed it at her. "You are a wonderful woman, my dear Adriana. If Slocum wasn't around, I'd hire a band and court you myself."

"All I need outside my window are four drunk Mexicans playing two different songs in the middle of the night." She shook her head, and then thanked the girl who brought her a plate of food.

"I can imagine." Slocum chuckled. What was he forgetting? Once they were south of Deming, there would be no stores or even villages for days. The Apaches had cleared all that country of small ranchers and town dwellers alike. Even most of the large rancheros sat empty—but there was also some dead land down there before they would reach the mountains. Barren alkali country without rainfall or watering holes for miles.

"Two water barrels," he said.

"Yes and some hemp rope," she said, and pointed for him to write it down.

"How many mules are they bringing?" Enrique asked.

"I don't know," she said. "Early this morning I sent a boy to tell this man I know to bring several head."

Slocum hugged her shoulder. "And after that you asked me if I was going?"

"Sure." She winked at him. "I could always send them back."

Dyke pointed his glass at her. "Now that's class. Real class in a lady. She thinks of everything and puts up with us scruffy characters in her great house to boot."

"We give baths, too."

Dyke rubbed the side of his whisker-stubbled face with his palm. "How many in the tub?"

They all laughed. She looked a bit embarrassed, reached out, and caught his arm. "Not with me."

Slocum shook his head. He would damn sure miss this place. Her, her body, her hospitality and humor.

Mules arrived, braying their heads off in a strange place. Slocum took his steaming coffee cup with him. She clung to his other arm and they went to see the animals.

"Sounds like an ample array of them out there," Dyke said. He stood up, downed the last of the contents in his glass, set it down, and headed for the front door.

Enrique was the first to shake the man's hand. Andrew Karnes, who spoke with a deep Southern drawl, shook hands with each of them and doffed his straw planter's hat for Adriana. He wore white cotton dress clothing that looked immaculate in the morning sun.

"There's twelve mules here," he said. "Stout, tall for mules in New Mexico. They came six weeks ago in a pack train from Silver City. Man delivered his bullion to Wells Fargo here, sold me the mules, then took the train to San Antonio."

"He have camping gear?" Slocum asked Karnes as

Dyke and the boy checked the mules over for age and soundness.

"Yes. They had a good outfit," Karnes said. "I have it for sale, too."

Adriana nodded her approval at Slocum.

"What's it worth?" he asked.

"A hundred," said Karnes.

"Twenty-five."

"You've not seen it, sir."

"Ten."

Karnes took his hat off and shook his head in defeat. "Ma'am, is he buying the mules, too?"

"Yes. I'll let him."

"Oh, my. I have ten dollars in each of those packsaddles and pads. I want fifteen each for them. I can sell them. There will be folks coming through here will need them. Each one has good leather and even some new girths I replaced. Ain't a gald on any of these mules' withers in this bunch."

Slocum agreed. "That number will depend on the mules we pick out."

Karnes agreed. "The whole camping outfit cost me fifty dollars. I want thirty profit."

"Seventy-five if it suits my cook."

"I'll have it all here before dark. You'll see it's well worth that."

"How many mules do we need?" Dyke asked, holding his elbow and squeezing his chin whiskers.

"Ten, if there are that many sound ones."

Dyke had Karnes's Mexican boys bring out the mules they'd selected. Slocum walked around them. Any Georgia farmer would have been proud to have owned a team of their like. They were almost too good to even consider taking onto the Madres. It would be a rough trip for any animal, but they looked stout enough.

"How much?" Slocum asked.

Karnes came and stood beside him. "I have lots of money in them."

Slocum never shook his head. "The man got here. Sent his bullion on by Wells Fargo and dumped these mules on you."

"Not exactly."

"No, I know that's the case."

"An army mule buyer comes by here—"

"He'd be lost."

"From Fort Bowie—"

"We ain't there."

"Take a hundred a head. They ain't getting no cheaper. You've done picked the best mules in the outfit."

"Fifty."

"No, sir, I'll take my mules and go back home."

"Get your trading pants on."

"I've got them on. I give you them saddles at a fair price."

"They're all over. Packsaddles are on every corral."

"Not all ready to go and good Navajo pads."

So their dickering continued through their noon lunch of roasted *carbito*. Enrique rode off to El Paso to find Buck Benton and then to meet the others at Deming. Adriana sat at Slocum's side at the great table through the fine meal, and looked both amused and pleased at his trading skills.

He'd finally bought the mules for seventy-five dollars. Supplies that Adriana had sent for were arriving. Dyke, aided by two of the house girls, was taking inventory of the camp gear Karnes had sent them.

"Better figure it out. We leave at sunup," Slocum told Dyke.

Adriana led Slocum off by the arm for a siesta.

Upstairs, with her linen curtains billowing in the warm breeze, she sat on a stuffed chair and undid the concho buttons up the side of her leather pants. He looked out the window at the cottonwoods down by the Rio Grande.

"Pull my boots off," she said, and held the right one up

for him to remove. Then he eased the left one off. "I am going to miss having you around here."

She stood up and began to peel the pants off her hips. "You are awfully quiet today."

He toed off his boots. "I am thinking, I guess, about those people and how we can help them lift Durango's yoke off of them."

"A crazy reporter, a has-been lawman, a boy, and you—my, my, what a fearsome army."

He glanced over and studied her long coffee-colored legs as she removed the pants off her feet. Hobbling around, she laughed. "I must be clumsy today."

He hung his gun belt on a wall peg, then walked across the room and began to undo the buttons on her fancy blouse with the ruffles. Their gaze met and he kissed her, still opening the treasure chest until he could fondle the long teardrop breasts in his hands. She squeezed his face between her palms and kissed him harder.

At last she tore her face from his and tears ran down her cheeks. "Get undressed and get in bed—now."

She undid his belt and shoved his pants down to his knees as he unbuttoned his shirt. When he was naked at last, she led him to the great feather bed and then, with both hands, pushed him over backward onto the sheet.

Then she climbed on top of him. Mischief was in her smile as she moved to straddle him. Above her, the white canopy made her coffee-colored body stand out. Her breasts swayed as she worked herself in place. Then rising up, she sucked in her slight tummy and began looking down intently as she inserted his dick in herself.

Soon she was riding his pole, bouncing off the bed. He raised his butt off the sheet to meet her. Then she lay flat on top of him, her hungry mouth feasting on his, working her nail-like clit on his shaft back and forth until she was heaving for breath with each hard hunch at him.

Then, sensing his final arousal approaching, she clutched

him tight and hard. He came and she cried out. It was one of two volleys that he gave her. They fell asleep in each other's arms—connected, with her sprawled on top of him.

Later, they bathed together in a great copper tub that her late husband had ordered for such occasions. He was probably squirming in his grave down at the Our Lady of Mercy Cemetery over Slocum sharing it with his widow. Slocum could only think of other baths he'd taken in icy horse tanks, mossy hot cow tanks, and Chinese bathhouses where the perfume stung his nose.

They kissed before the water turned too cold, and ended back in bed for a quick session.

She put on a fancy red velvet dress for supper, and he shaved, then dressed in some clothes that she bought him. A starched white shirt with a collar, pressed cotton pants, and a suit coat made of light tan canvas. He was certain few would even recognize him in this attire as he buttoned up the back of the dress for her. After pinning up her hair, she added a sparkling diamond necklace.

"Anyone coming for supper?" he asked, putting the shawl on her shoulders at the door.

"I guess the reporter. I didn't want to share you on our last night."

He laughed. She didn't even smirk—he knew she was serious.

The next morning in the predawn, the mules were braying in protest as everyone hustled about to get them loaded and ready for the road. Dyke had searched the provisions over and over to be certain everything was in its proper place. Slocum and Adriana threw a diamond hitch over a mule Dyke certified as ready.

Leaving never was easy—especially with such an unselfish woman. He finished the final tie, whirled around, and hugged her about over backward until she pulled her boots up behind her butt and laughed out loud at his antics.

"Thanks for all your help," he said.

"I knew after you went to sleep each night that I was living in a dream world, but I enjoyed it. In fact, I won't forget it." She shook her head. "Oh, I didn't want you to leave and me not be here."

She sniffed. "I told them to saddle that dun horse for you. He is my special gift. I want you to have him."

"You've done too much already for an old cowboy riding the chuck line."

"Take him and think of me when you ride back this way. I'll always be here with all of my late husband's money and ranches, I hope."

He walked her to the yard and looked at the fine gelding standing at the hitch rail. Then he nodded and stepped in the stirrup, seeing that Dyke was ready to go. The dun was anxious and stepped around, forcing Adriana to back up. He blew her a kiss and she returned it.

"*Vaya con Dios*, my love."

3

The woman standing before Durango was Señora Valdez. He peeked up at her from under his sombrero. The sun was a little too bright this morning. His head hurt badly.

At the sight of her, he shoved the hat back on his shoulders and sat up straight. Such a voluptuous woman. Madre de Dios, why didn't they tell him it was her?

"What can I do for you, Señora?"

She stood there in a plain brown dress. But nothing was plain about her. The rise and fall of her breasts under the material gave him an erection. Copperlike coins on chains were draped around her neck and trailed down past her willowy hips. That was her only jewelry. It would look like nothing on some *puta,* but on her it looked fabulously rich.

"Some of your men have stolen some of my goats," she said.

"My men?" He drove a thumb in his chest. "Oh, you must be mistaken about my men stealing your goats."

"You can make fun of me if you like. They said you were the mayor and the man in charge. Is there nothing you can do about them stealing my goats?"

He didn't want her to leave—she was so beautiful. What must he do to keep her there?

"Are you certain it is not a coyote?" He began conniving on how to get her in his bed. Mercy sakes, she would be such a prize.

"A two-legged one. Maybe three of them."

"But why would my men steal goats from you? No one else complains about that."

She folded her arms over her chest. "No, they are all afraid of you."

"What have I done to deserve this?"

"Murdered those innocent children the other day."

He glared hard at her. The muscles in his face drew tighter. "That woman helped her husband murder one of my men." He squeezed his fist at her and spoke through his teeth. "She wouldn't tell me where he was hidden. She killed those children, and I will find him and I will kill him, too. No one—no one kills my men and gets away with it."

"Maybe I feel the same about my goats."

He threw his head back and laughed. "You are a very funny woman. Where is your husband, Señora Valdez?"

"He works in mines. He builds elevators and lifts things up and down in mine shafts."

"What mine is he working at now?"

She shrugged. "I never ask."

"You must come see me more often, Señora Valdez."

"Will it stop them from eating my goats?"

He smiled. "Come back again and we can talk about it some more."

"Thank you." She gave him a nod and then turned to leave.

He watched her gracefully walking toward the stream. There she shed her sandals and, holding her dress tail up with one hand, waded across the ford. Soon she disappeared into the cottonwoods.

Leaning back in the chair, he drew a deep breath. "Tomas."

"*Sí*, Captain?" The man was standing behind him.

"Tell those dumb sons of a bitches eating her goats to quit."

"*Sí*, Captain."

"Did you send someone to see about Lupe?"

"*Sí*, Captain."

"What did you learn?"

"They said she was sitting on some pillows and moaning about her sore ass."

He laughed and shook his head. Such a big baby. And not nearly as elegant as this Valdez woman. She made him horny just thinking about her.

"Tell the women to come back and wash their clothes in this part of the river. No one is to bother them. I miss them doing that. Most of them do it bare-breasted and they are fun to watch."

"They will be back, Captain."

"Good—there was a girl here last night dancing in the cantina. They call her Marisel."

"Do you wish her?"

"Yes, she might be interesting to talk to this afternoon."

"I will send someone to find her."

"Tomas, invite her the first time."

"*Sí*, Captain."

He looked at the sky for help. He had to tell them everything.

"One more thing, Captain."

"What is that?"

"The Contreras boy who went to sleep at his guard post."

"Bring all those not on guard duty here to the cantina at five o'clock. He will receive twenty lashes for his first offense, but all of them must see it."

"*Sí*, Captain."

Durango reached back and retrieved his sombrero to put on his head and shade his eyes from that too bright sun. He had to schedule the guard duty at each end of the valley. The passes on the east and the south were the only ways in and out off the valley unless you were a mountain goat.

He rotated the men on guard duty every five days, except in the east, where a good man named Mateo was in charge and stayed at that post all the time. One experienced man and two others at each post. That gave them all plenty of time for fandangos and hell-raising. It was better than being in prison, but some did not understand—they all had to maintain their security in this place.

So far he had lost three men—they would be hard to replace. Maybe he could drop to two men at each post. No, he needed more soldiers, but getting them would not be easy. These men he had known in prison, but many others in prison could not be trusted to work outside.

Seventeen men plus Tomas and himself—it concerned him. But he did have some other resources. There was a large supply of blasting material he'd taken from two pack trains headed for mines in the Madres. And an ample amount of money in coins that he'd robbed from a government mint. Plus a Gatling gun that he'd brought in in pieces and stored in a secured vault.

All were things he could use against the forces that might try to end his rule.

He was getting up from his siesta when he saw the girl seated crossed-legged on his floor. After a look at her in the shadowy light, he rubbed his face with his hands. He'd slept too hard. He needed to focus. Now this light-toed dancer was there.

"Marisel, right?" He studied her.

"*Sí, señor.*"

He rose and went to the door to cough up the phlegm in his throat and spit it out on the ground. With his forearm braced on the door facing, he noticed some of the washerwomen were back at the river. "You are from the village?"

"Yes, I have never been away from here."

He walked back to sit on the bed again. "You have no husband?"

"Oh, no."

"They must be blind not to see your beauty."

She blushed and tried to dismiss the compliment. "There are many pretty women in this valley."

"Yes, there are." Maybe he could talk her into getting on the bed. "You know I can grant many favors?"

"Oh, yes, you are the mayor."

"Then come and sit with me and tell me about your life." He patted the bed beside him.

She looked around and then shrugged. "I don't know."

"Oh, my bed is much softer to sit on than that hard floor." He stuck out his arm to help her up.

She nodded. "But I don't think—"

"Why not? I am the mayor. I could order you to sit by me."

She snickered and covered her mouth with her long graceful hands. "All right."

He felt relieved. His seduction of Marisel was going fine. He must control his impatience and his lust to get in her crotch. With her bouncing on her butt beside him testing the bed—he knew that he would have his way with her in a short time.

"Captain? Captain?" Tomas called out.

Damn, what was wrong? "Excuse me?" he said to Marisel.

"Sure," she said, kicking her legs back and forth.

He hurried to the door. "What is it?" he hissed at his man.

"The Yaqui—the one called Snake—has some rebels trapped in the lower canyon. He sent a boy for you to come and wipe them out."

"How many?"

"I have no idea."

"Get all the men you can. This may be our chance to eliminate all our troubles once and for all."

"I will have your horse here in a few minutes. The boy has gone for him."

"Very good. We must be swift."

"I will hurry."

"Use the trumpet player in the cantina. That will be a faster way to get the men here."

"*Sí*, Captain."

He went back inside. "My little one, I must leave you."

"There is trouble?" She jumped up to her feet as the trumpeter began to sound the call.

"A small matter that needs my attention. I am sorry."

"Will you return soon?"

"I am not sure. Sleep in my big bed when you are tired. I have no idea when I will return to you, little one."

"Be careful." She chewed on her lip.

He swept her up and kissed her. Her eyes fluttered when he set her down. "I hear my horse. I must go now."

Her fingers covered her mouth as if he'd burned it. She nodded. "*Vaya con Dios*."

He nodded, squared his shoulders, and went outside. Men leading and riding horses were coming from all directions. He mounted Eagle and whirled around in a full circle. The horse's long dark mane flared out like a great skirt in a dance. In his doorway stood his dancer, who waved to him.

"Tomas, we must go. You bring the others."

"*Sí*, Captain."

He rushed down the trail beside the stream. Riding his great stallion was like harnessing the winds. The day was fast dying—they needed to be swift or the night would swallow them. He reined up before the Yaqui, who was standing on a house-sized rock with a rifle in the crook of his arm.

"Snake, where are they?"

Snake pointed. "Trapped. They can't get out."

"You circle around to the top and pick them off if you can."

"Take much time to get up there."

"We'll do all the shooting down here. Hurry, get up there."

Shots from the rebels began to ricochet around them. He and his men had to take cover in the timber. These devils would die hard. He didn't dare send some of his men into the canyon—he could not afford to lose any of them.

On their bellies, they crept closer in the twilight, risking a shot now and then at where they supposed the rebels were, then taking fast cover. Edging his way nearer, Durango kept hearing a high-pitched whine over his head. What was that sound?

The stars were coming out, but the mountain's face looked dark. Then he saw the basket swing out.

"They are using a winch to escape!"

Shots thudded into the basket. Then it fell and crashed on the ground. The outlaws rushed over and someone struck a light. Durango discovered the dead man in the basket was Snake, his scout. Damn.

"Captain, what shall we do?"

"Bury him." Durango shook his head wearily. "We will curse the loss of him."

"Who did this?"

"Señora Valdez's husband." No need to explain anything. Her man was an engineer of this sort—he lifted people in and out of mines.

4

The road followed the railroad tracks westward. Congress
had given the Southern Pacific every other section, one on
the left, then one on the right, to help pay for the railroad's
track-building costs. Most of these checkerboard plots were
sold to big investors. Slocum and Dyke kept seeing the
WWK brand on things like pens and mills. There were water wells that no doubt had been drilled by the SP during the
railroad's construction.

By late afternoon, they were in the open grassland that
was surrounded at a distance by jagged ranges of purple
mountains. Slocum felt they were almost halfway to
Deming.

"Here, hold the lead on this bell mare," Slocum said,
and the red-faced Dyke booted his mule up close. He'd
spent all day in the rear driving the mules to make them
keep up.

"I may hire a mule beater in Deming," Dyke said.

"Enrique can do that."

"Yes, yes, he can do that."

"I'm going to ride over and speak to someone at that
house about using the shipping pens for holding our stock
tonight."

"Yes, that way we might have those mules here in the morning."

"Handier. I doubt they'll leave that bell mare." Slocum rode over, and a short young woman came to the doorway.

He dismounted and removed his hat. "Ma'am, we need to camp for the night. May we water our stock and put them in the pens overnight? I can pay you."

"Go ahead. They aren't my pens anyway."

"You work for the ranch?"

"No, but Frisco does."

"He must be your man—Frisco?"

She nodded. "Where are you going?"

"Mexico."

"That is a big country."

"Really we're going to the Madres."

She nodded. Wearing a many-layered skirt and simple blouse, she looked like a lot of other border women of mixed ancestry. In her twenties, she still could smile and show some spunk. With no big breasts and no belly, she looked much younger than her age.

She dropped her gaze and moved her bare toes on her right foot back and forth over the threshold. "I can cook. Take me with you."

"I'd have to check with my other partners in Deming."

"What would one woman matter?"

"I have no spare horse."

"I can find a burro to ride."

"Whatever. But I have to warn you they may object to a woman going along."

She shrugged. "I can go that far anyway."

"Fine." He started to mount up and she went back inside. Maybe she'd changed her mind about going along. No matter. He had lots to do and the day was waning.

He rode back to tell Dyke. "She said we can use the pens, they don't belong to her."

"Good, I was for using them anyway." He was busy undoing the first hitch. They were halfway through unloading all the packs when a donkey began braying from afar at the mules.

"She got a burro?" Dyke asked, looking up.

"Said she had one."

"She's got one."

In a short time, the woman joined them on a burro with a blanket roll and a small valise that was all scuffed and so worn from wear that she used sea-grass string to tie it shut. Two gunnysacks stuffed full of sticks were also slung across the burro's back. She jumped down with a show of brown legs and led the burro inside the pen. Once the gate was closed, she put down her roll and case and swung the sacks off the burro's back. He spooked a little, but she let him go off dragging his halter rope. That was all she had to ride him with.

"I can build a fire for the meal or help you unload." She stood there with her hands on her small hips appraising things.

"Cook," Dyke said, and wrestled another pannier off the sawbuck.

"What do you have to eat?" she asked.

"The food's over here," Slocum said, pointing to a pannier on that end. "Flour, sugar, lard, salt pork, frijoles, rice, raisins, jerky. We got it all."

"What if I make some biscuits and gravy tonight and then cook some frijoles all night for breakfast?"

"Hmm," Dyke said, taking a breather and looking hard at her. "You sure you know how to make biscuits and gravy?"

"Sure. I told him I was a cook."

Slocum chuckled over their bantering. "That sounds good 'cause we planned on sharpening our teeth on some jerky for supper."

She laughed. "Can I fix coffee?"

"Yes," they both shouted.

When the mules were finally unpacked, Slocum and Dyke

dropped on the ground near her small but hot fire. She squatted next to it, busy feeding it small sticks to keep the blaze going under her pots. The one Dutch oven baking the bread was covered in red hot ashes. In the skillet, her gravy made of flour and canned milk was thickening in blobs.

"My name is Doña," she said, and fluffed her hair while balancing on her toes.

"He's Slocum and I'm Dyke."

"Nice to meet you. You have good equipment for a cook to use."

"Fair stuff anyway. That old man ain't coming home tonight, is he?" Dyke asked.

"No." She shook her head as if it was silly to ask. "He makes a long circuit checking their cattle."

"He treat you all right?" Dyke asked.

She shrugged in the growing twilight.

"I guess I knew the answer with you running off with us."

"I wanted to go back to the mountains. He said he would take me. That's why I came out here." Her eyes narrowed. "Then one day I knew he was not going to take me there."

She got up and used the hook to turn her lid on the Dutch oven halfway around over the bread. "It will be ready soon."

Slocum found a candle lamp in a wooden case among the provisions and lit the wick. It reflected a lot of light, and its brass trim and glass sides gleamed. "Very fancy light so you can see."

"My, you two have some operation," she said.

"Don't get no ideas," Dyke said, making a sweep. "We borrowed all this stuff."

She laughed.

They ate her biscuits and gravy until they about busted. Washed it down with the rich coffee she roasted—not one taste of burned beans in any of it.

Slocum offered to help her wash dishes. She dismissed

his offer and said she had beans to sort and the two men should go off to bed.

He shook out his bedroll and kicked the knots and things away from the spot he'd chosen, then removed his run-down boots and britches and lay down. A thousand stars pricked the sky, and he soon rolled over and went to sleep.

He never knew when she slipped into his bedroll, but she was shivering and her icy flesh against his warm skin made him roll over and hug her. She warmed her small cold hand, rubbing it up and down on his leg.

"Damn, you about froze," he said in her ear.

Hunching her shoulder, she said, "I should have took two blankets."

"Hell, maybe three. Where did all that daytime temperature go?"

She moved his hand on top of her teacup breast. "It always gets cold up here at night."

He soon was warming the pair of them. And they tasted each other's mouths, growing headier by the moment. Then she slipped under him and eased his dick inside. It was a slow and pleasureable enough pace, and her cold legs and feet soon warmed. Finally, she raised her butt to meet him, and sighed deeply when he came. Snuggled close, they fell back asleep.

Wood smoke woke him. Then he realized it was almost dawn and she was gone. He rose in the cold air and pulled on his pants. Boots on, he went by to wake Dyke, and then stepped off a ways to piss. Then he returned, swept up his hat and gun belt.

"You two want some coffee?" she asked. "Before you start?"

"I never drink the damn stuff, but yours was so damn good last night I'll have another cup," Dyke said, and joined her as she squatted underneath a blanket over her shoulders while tending the fire.

"This is fresh," she said, and laughed.

With only Slocum and Dyke to catch and saddle everything, they were over an hour arguing with mules and reloading them.

"Be nice to have help next time," Dyke said when they
walked back to camp. All they had left to load were the
food boxes.

"I don't care. Deming can wait. I'm eating my fill of
beans," Slocum said, sitting down cross-legged and taking
a heaping plate she offered him with a folded flour tortilla
to use for a utensil. By damn, he thought, she'd made them
that morning, too.

"I have biscuits left to keep you full today," she said. "I
usually put raisins in the last batch for the next day. I'll do
better later."

Slocum waved his tortilla at her. "You done good, girl,
real good."

"Hell, yes, she did," said Dyke. "If I wasn't still married
to a hussy in Connecticut. I'd make you my bride."

"You've got a wife?" Slocum about choked on his mouth-
ful of beans. "Hell, I never knew you were married."

"Lily Dale Carpenter was her maiden name. My family arranged the marriage with someone of proper social
standing and wealth. A rather horse-faced old girl who would
not let me culminate our wedding in the New York Astor Hotel bed, because she feared the blood from severing her virginity would leave a telltale stain on the sheets for all the staff
to know about what we'd been doing, and thus she would be
unable to face them even in the halls."

Slocum and Doña about rolled on the ground laughing.

"Well, Dyke, tell us, did you do the deed?"

"Hell, yes, and there was no blood—about like poking a
stick in clabbered milk." He dropped his head and shook it.
"I'd almost forgotten her."

"No divorce?"

He looked up at the two of them. "Why, lands, no. It
would scandalize the family name. I left before the first an-

niversary. Went off to war. Came home on the train after Appomattox. Got back there early one morning and decided to see what my loving wife was doing."

"Well?" Slocum asked.

"I crept up to her bedroom quietlike to wake my wedded wife and perhaps arouse some spousal sympathy from her to give me a union with her. Me being a celebrated war hero and a major.

"I swung open the door, and there she was on her hands and knees on the polished hardwood floor with that skinny German butler playing the role of the stud dog. I must say, he was some kind of a stage actor, too. Any dog would have been proud of him."

"Oh, Dyke, that is so sad," Doña said.

"I have laughed about it many times since, my dear."

"Deming is calling, folks. Let's ride."

"Pray tell, Doña, didn't Mr. Lincoln turn all the slaves loose?"

"Not free, Dyke, just loose."

Slocum went for the dun horse. They had a long day's ride ahead. They could rest when they got there. U.S. Army Major Dyke Von Schultz. Slocum learned something new every day.

5

Marisel was not at the cantina when Durango returned around midnight, nor was she in his bed. That made him angry. Too tired to do anything about it, he dropped on the bed, still dressed, and soon slept. Groggy the next morning from sleeping so hard, he went to the doorway to piss on the flat cactus pads beside the door.

There were more women washing clothes in the river. He smiled at the colorful splash of their different-colored dresses on the far side of the silver stream along with some gleaming brown skin and bare breasts. His man Tomas had gotten the word out—good. If only the rest were so easy to do.

He shook off his stem and put it away. Where had the girl gone? Strange that she had left. And Señora Valdez— he must talk to her some more about her husband the engineer. Those rebels needed to be stopped. If they weren't, they would gain support among the others. Trouble, trouble, when all he wanted to do was screw a few nice women and have a good life. He needed more men, too, but who could he trust?

Maybe he could recruit them among the village

population. Money bought lots of things in a society that hardly knew what it was—the villagers bartered for most things.

He went through the side door from his room into the empty cantina. Nalda, the bar maid, nodded when she saw him. "I will make you some food."

With a nod, he went to one of the few chairs and dropped onto it. The place stank of old smoke, liquor, and body musk. More like an unwiped ass.

She brought him a steaming mug of coffee. "Here, Captain. There is no milk."

He waved her away. And he dared a sip. Hot as hell, but the vapors went up his nose and revived him. She still stood there. He nodded his approval and she spun around.

Skinny-assed and well-used, she held no appeal for him. He'd messed with her when he first returned, but he'd as soon use a hole bored in a board as stick it to her. At least the lumber would be a tight fit.

Tomas must be sleeping in. Maybe Durango could hire four local men to work shifts at the guard posts, and one of his best would be in charge of them at each place. That would free up some of his men—they'd like that. But he had to be careful or he'd have some of the rebels as guards.

No problem, he'd give his man in charge the order to shoot anyone who looked cross-eyed. So that was solved. Nalda brought him some black beans, eggs, red salsa, and several flour tortillas.

"I will refill your coffee," she announced, and gave him a bump on the arm with her skinny butt before she left to refill it.

She must not have gotten laid the night before. He filled the first wrap with the mixture, and the saliva began to flow in his mouth in anticipation. Recalling the tasteless meals of recooked mashed frijoles slapped on a tin plate in prison, he chewed every bite of her cooking and allowed the taste and flavor to saturate his mouth.

"Captain?"

He glanced up and saw Tomas coming in the room. With his mouth full, he indicated the other chair with his wrap. Finally, he spoke to Nalda, who was back behind the bar. "Bring him some food and coffee."

"*Sí,* Captain." And she was gone.

"The women are back," said Durango. "I saw them in the river this morning."

Tomas beamed and nodded.

Between bites, Durango explained his plan for hiring guards from the locals. Tomas agreed, and then his breakfast arrived.

"So look for ones you feel are not rebels," said Durango.

"*Sí,* Captain."

"Enjoy your food," Durango said, pointing at his plate. "Remember how bad it was in prison."

"I never think of that." Tomas shook his head and began building a wrap. "Those days were worse than what Hell will ever be like."

"You ever wish to go back to that village where you were born?"

"And ride in on a shiny horse?" Tomas smiled as he prepared to take his first bite.

"What would you do next?"

"Have a feast for all the children in the town."

Durango blew on his coffee's steam. "Why that?"

"Because I remember going to bed at night so hungry and my stepfather whipping me for crying about it."

Closing his eyes, Durango nodded. "That is how I learned to steal. It was that or starve for me and my mother. I even let an old man fondle me once for some burritos. I see why you would feed them. What else would you do if you went back?"

Tomas's laughter was loud. "I would find Dolores, the prettiest girl in the whole village, and screw her silly."

"But what if she was old, fat, and ugly?"

"I would still do it because she spurned me for another.

If she had accepted me, I'd've been a poor farmer with many children." He laughed.

Durango wiped his mouth on his sleeve. "I can't see you as a farmer."

With imaginary plow handles in his hands, Durango rocked back and forth like he was making a furrow. Amused, he threw his hands up. "Wouldn't they all be surprised to see us?"

"Yes," Tomas said. "It would be a day to remember."

Slouched in the chair, Durango drummed his fingernails on the tabletop. "You hear any rumors?"

Wiping up the last of the salsa on his plate with the tortilla, Tomas looked up. "You mean about Slocum coming?"

"*Sí,* or anything else?"

"No. It is like they aren't talking about his return. Nothing in the last week."

Durango stared out the door at the water of the stream rushing by like time. No word might mean they could not find him, or that they knew he was coming back and dared not speak about it. "Listen close. Nalda, heat some water and shave me."

She ran off to obey his command.

"Send word to Señora Valdez I wish to see her."

"When do you want her to be here?"

He frowned. "I mean invite her."

"*Sí,* Captain."

When Nalda finished shaving him, he studied his face in the small hand mirror. No cuts. She did good. As she swished the blade in the basin of water, she looked ready to ask him something.

"Clean my room. Air my bedding and wash the sheets. I want it to smell like—juniper. You know what I mean?"

"But—"

"Hire some girls to do it. Here are their wages." He put three ten-centavo pieces on the table.

When she reached for them, he caught her hand in a tight clasp. "They are for the girls."

She spun around to look at him like an angry fussed cat ready to spit.

In his other hand, he produced a shiny silver cartwheel that gleamed. It was so new, he felt the sharp serrated edges that cut into even his callused fingertips. "This—is for you."

Her dark face became aglow and she hugged his neck. "I love you so much."

Sure, for a dollar she'd do anything, including screw an army. *The little bitch.* "Don't waste any time."

"No, Captain." She put the folded razor in her apron pocket, swept the basin and towel away, and with a swish of her skirt went off.

"You wish some pulque?" José asked from behind the bar. The man must have just arrived. He slept in the village across the stream or in a hammock outside now that Durango had taken over his room.

"Ah, yes," said Durango.

"Did you get those rebels last night?"

Durango frowned. Was José not there in the bar when he and his men returned? "No, they slipped away from us."

José delivered his mug, with froth running over the lip. "They are like shadows, no?"

"But a bullet between the eyes even kills shadows, huh?"

"Oh, *sí.* The corn man should be here today."

"No short measures," Durango warned him.

"This man is honest as a padre."

"Ha, they are men, too. They steal and lie, too."

José nodded.

Durango raised his mug for his first sip, and listened to the women in the side room sounding like a flock of magpies feasting on a dead steer.

"Close the door," he told José, who hurried to do so.

Durango took his mug to the front door to escape the racket. With his shoulder against the facing, he watched the washerwomen on the far bank. The only problem was that at this distance, he could not see any women with nice titties showing.

Sipping his sour drink, he wondered about Señora Valdez. She would come like a princess, take her steer-hide thongs off at the water with such delicate movements, standing upright. Then she'd raise her skirt above the rushing water, cross like it was nothing, and reach the other side—damn, even that picture made his dick hard.

In a short while, he was back lounging under the shade of the grape arbor. The strong south wind swept away the sweat that came from under his hatband. Where was that bastard Slocum? He looked at the peaks rising in the east—he'd break Slocum in two with his bare hands this time.

After his siesta, he stopped in the doorway and blinked in disbelief. He saw Señora Valdez, and wondered why he had not changed his clothes. She was crossing the water, calmly holding her skirt up. What a great lady. He needed such a woman when he established his ranchero. These damn Apaches could not forever hold all this land in Sonora. The gringos were after them, even in Mexico.

When she stopped at the end of the arbor, he made a bow. "Good day, Señora."

"Good day yourself, Mayor."

"Ah, it was so nice of you to accept my invitation to come by and visit with me."

"I guess if it saves my goats, that is reward enough."

He laughed aloud, holding the chair for her. When she was seated, he asked her, "Would you like some wine?"

"That would be rather nice."

"I will order us some."

"Don't go to any trouble."

"No trouble. No trouble at all." He excused himself and stepped to the door of the cantina. "Some good wine, a glass, and a mug of pulque for me."

He sat at the table. "Such a nice day, huh?"

"Yes, but these children I see need to be in school. They need to learn to read and write. Education is important."

"*Sí*, are you a teacher?"

"No, not really. I have an education, but no, I am not a teacher."

Nalda brought the wine and his drink on a tray. She poured Señora Valdez a glass and set the bottle on the table. He kept thinking about her legs under that full pleated skirt. He'd like to run his palms over them.

"I see," he said to the señora. "You know, children should be children. They should run and play. Be free. I don't think that it is so bad."

"Bad? They can do that after they learn to read and write."

He rubbed the side of his index finger over his upper lip. "Is there a school here?"

"Yes, there is an old building to serve as one."

"They ever have a teacher here?"

"Once two years ago, but there was no money to pay him so he left."

"So you want a school again, no?" He settled back in his chair.

"Yes, I do, and you are the man who can help us."

He closed his eyes. His few days spent in a classroom carried a horrible memory. He went there to learn to read—after a week, he still did not know how to read, but his hands hurt from being slapped so many times with a stick by a sourpuss nun. All for offenses she found him guilty of. His fingernails were dirty. His hair had not been brushed that morning. Once because he farted—he was supposed to hold it during class.

"How could I help you?" he asked.

"Get a teacher."

"Would you teach in this school?"

Her dark eyes cut around and met his gaze. "You are serious?"

He turned up his palms. "I am as serious as can be."

"I would need some books and chalk and paper and pencils."

He waved that off. "Make a list and tomorrow we can go over it."

"You aren't just saying this?"

"You want a school, I can help you, no?"

Her warm smile and smug nod made his dick harder in his pants. He could trade all that list for one piece of her ass. She wanted a school, he wanted her. They could reach an agreement.

Already, he felt better. "Where is this schoolhouse?"

"It is up the side road on the right. There is a faded sign on it."

He liked to see her excited. She looked ready to do a dance as she sat across from him, sipping on her wine. He had done many things, but a school would be different. Ordinary men did many things to get some pussy—he'd never thought of it before like this.

6

The locomotive whistles in the night spooked the mules, and they crowded Deming's Main Street boardwalk to get away from the tracks that were on the other side of the street. Men cussed them, and Slocum gave a cross look back at anyone who did so.

"Leave them mules alone. They'll kick your damn head off," he shouted at one drunk bastard waving his hat at them. Besides, Slocum didn't need them to stampede. They were loose following the bell mare and after such a long hard day on the road, he'd never expected for them to be so upset.

With some urging of Blanco, Dyke rode his mule onto the boardwalk to herd the other mules back toward the street and closer to all the train-switching activity that had gotten them so upset. His rusty voice cut the night, and Slocum saw him swing his knotted rope at some loudmouth bystander who was cussing him out. The clatter of the white mule's hooves scrambling on the wood told Slocum that Dyke was cutting a path for himself.

A block ahead, Slocum saw the sign for the livery and shouted, "We're about there."

"Good. Get over, you damn mules." Dyke swung his

rope at the pack animals crowding him. "Them trains ain't about to bite you."

"Get them gawdamn mules off the sidewalk," someone demanded.

"What in the hell do you think we're trying to do?" Slocum stood in the stirrup to see who was giving them orders.

A shotgun-toting marshal in a long-tail black coat and a high-crown black hat stepped into the open, holding his scattergun like he was ready to fire it. It was all that Slocum needed.

He put spurs to the dun horse and drove him toward the man, sliding him hard on his heels. "Fire that gun and it may be the last thing you ever do."

"Who the fuck are you?" The marshal raised the barrel and swung it around menacingly.

"We're a half block from having these mules off your street. Now step aside and let us do our job. Firing that Greener off is only going to make things tougher when the mules bust loose and stampede."

"Listen, I'm the law here." He blinked as Doña drove her burro past him with unexpected speed. "She with you, too?"

"I guess so. Now move aside so them mules don't get a notion to go in one of them saloons and kick hell out of everything."

The marshal hesitated for a second, then stepped back. Meanwhile, the mules had sent a few horses hitched at the racks into a fit and spooked them backward. But Dyke was getting the mules under control. They began to file out into the street after the lead mare, her copper bell clanking in the night. The dun moved up the street in his swinging walk with the lead mare in tow.

Doña stood in the street beside the open gate to the pen, waving her arms to direct them. Slocum nodded and gave her a grin as he rode past her on the single-footing dun. Dyke was last to ride in, and she shut the gate.

A familiar mustached face appeared on the top rail. "Hell, Slocum, you about rousted the town law and all Deming getting here with them hee-haws."

"Buck," he said, dismounting heavily. "We were having enough hell. We damn sure didn't need him shooting that scattergun."

"You brought all this?" Enrique asked from beside Buck.

"Hell, Slocum always goes top class, boy," Buck said.

"Get your asses off that fence and help us unpack," Dyke grumbled.

"Who's this gate-opening gal?" Buck took off his hat for Doña with a short bow.

"Doña, meet Buck Benton. Buck, go clear this with the liveryman. I'm damn tired and ready for bed."

"You can say that for me, too." Dyke was circling around bent over and holding his hips.

Buck made the deal with the liveryman. After the mules were unloaded, Enrique agreed to stay and guard the panniers while the others went up the street to the café for a meal. Slocum knew he couldn't leave their supplies unguarded in a wide-open place like this town. An around-the-clock guard would be necessary until they were back on the road.

The meal served them was typical hash, and Dyke told Buck that Doña could outcook the café with one hand.

She blushed under his praise. "Well, maybe."

"No maybe. We're going to spend two nights here," Slocum said. "The mules need the rest. We pushed them hard today to get here and they have a tough way ahead. I want our things guarded night and day. You two and Enrique figure it out."

"We can do that," Buck said.

"I'll see you tomorrow. What hotel has the fewest bedbugs?"

"Palace."

Rising from the chair, Slocum threw down the money to pay for their meal.

"Come on, Doña. We'll go find you some duds and a bath." He paused and looked at Buck. "Tomorrow, buy her a short horse and saddle. That damn burro won't make it. She beat half his ass off today."

Dyke started coughing and laughing. "She damn sure did."

A block away, Slocum opened the glass-windowed door to a store.

She gave him a perplexed look as she followed him inside.

"These canvas pants shrink, so you buy them a size big and wear galluses. A pullover shirt, and how about boots if they have your size?"

She turned up her palms and looked lost.

"We can work it out. Don't worry."

"May I help you?" a young clerk said.

"Find her a pair of them good canvas pants. A size too big. They'll shrink." They followed him down the rows of stacked, new-smelling clothing and brogan shoes.

"We *always* recommend at least one size bigger." The clerk stopped and handed him a pair off the shelf.

Slocum held them up to her waist. They would swallow her. "Next size."

"They were long, too," she whispered.

"Hell, we can cuff them or trim that off." He took the second pair, and after appraising them for size by holding the pants up, he said, "Try them on."

She stuffed her legs in them and worked them up until her feet stuck out. Then she bent over and pulled them up, wiggling to get them on under her dress.

Then she held them out from her waist. "Lots of room."

"Yeah, but they'll shrink front and back, too." Slocum turned to see the uncomfortable red-faced youth looking at the tin ceiling tiles. "We'll take 'em. Now we need a man's collarless pull-on shirt."

"Yes—sir." He acted anxious to go after one.

"What's the matter with him?" she whispered, wiggling the pants down.

He leaned over and spoke in her ear. "He ain't used to looking at a real woman dressing."

"Oh." She giggled. "I never thought about that, I was so excited about getting my new clothes."

"Don't try on the shirt. He might faint."

Going up the aisle behind Slocum, she hit him in the back. "Silly."

The blue shirt looked large, too. But she took it and the red galluses the clerk brought out.

"You have any boots to fit her?" Slocum lifted her up by the waist and set her on the counter.

She reached down and brushed off her soles, then sat there looking uncomfortable, swinging her feet while the clerk went to look for boots.

The boy produced a box. "These were special made for a lady who never came to get them," the clerk said. "I can give you a good price."

Slocum put his finger to his mouth and whispered, "Not a word to her."

"Why?"

"She might think they were a dead woman's shoes."

"Hmm, that may be why we haven't sold them." They went back to the counter.

She hopped off, slipped her foot in the boot, and put it on the floor. Slocum watched her. "Those were made to size," he said.

"Yes. But I don't know how they should feel."

He chuckled. "If they aren't too tight and you can stand them, they're fine."

The clerk was on the floor, pressing to find her toes and foot. "They fit you good."

She began chewing on her lower lip. "I don't know—"

"What's wrong?"

"I am about to cry." She pulled Slocum by the sleeve up

close to her and buried her wet face on his arm. "No one has ever been this kind to me before."

"Lordy, you've missed a lot, girl." She bent over and pulled on the other boot.

"You satisfied?" he asked her.

A little shaky, she walked down the aisle and back with her straw sombrero bouncing on her shoulders. Her heels were clacking. She threw back her head and then with both hands, moved her hair from her face. "They are so lovely."

He paid the clerk and, with the new clothes and boots in a large poke, they strolled toward the Palace. He stopped her at the front door of the New China Bathhouse. "I could use a bath. How about you?"

"Yes, before I wear those new clothes. Can I go in there?"

"You got money, you can." He laughed and pushed her toward the door.

She shook her head, amused. Holding the purchases in his left hand, he opened the door and she went in first.

"No ladies, no ladies," the short Chinese man behind the counter began repeating, as if that would make her leave.

"Listen, we need a bath and I've got the money to pay for it," said Slocum.

"No ladies 'llowed."

"You ain't listening. We need a bath."

"All right—all right. But can't insure her safe-ity."

"My gun will," he said.

"Put up screen. Maybe men want bath."

"Fine."

"Be twenty cent. Ten cent more clean you clothes."

"I'll take the whole thing. Watch her packages." He handed them to the man to stow.

In minutes, the folding screens were stood up around them in the damp-smelling bathhouse. Hot water was brought in buckets by three Chinese girls. Under their silk kimonos, they wore thick wooden-soled shoes and made a shuffling noise on the slatted floor.

He hung his gun belt on the ladder chair. Doña looked around, wrinkled her nose, and undid the strings at her waist. She stepped out of her skirt, showing her coffee-colored legs and compact bottom. Then she took the blouse off over her head and sighed. When her clothing was piled on the chair, she stepped into the left-hand tub.

"Whew, this is hot." Then she lowered herself into the steaming water, swallowing hard as the water level reached her small breasts.

"It'll relax you," he said, and stepped into his tub. Hot was a weak word for it, but he lowered himself in the caul-dron expecting to boil his most private parts.

The water soon felt comfortable, and he noticed she was busy soaping herself. As he did the same, his tight back muscles loosened some. They had passed a test that evening with the mules—only coming under attack might be worse. He'd have halter ropes tied to each mule so they could be recovered in case of such an incident happening again.

"My first bath," she said, and laughed. "In a bathhouse. I guess real ladies don't frequent these places?"

"You're a real lady. Those Chinese are scared they'll get in trouble with the law letting a female in, and then they'd get sent back home."

"Mules can get the law riled, too. I hope the marshal don't learn that I am in here." They both laughed.

One of the girls had taken their clothing, so they were trapped there until their garments were returned. Buckets to rinse themselves were delivered, and Slocum thanked the girls.

Another girl returned with robes for them to wear. "Clothes soon be ready." She bowed and went out.

In another half hour, they registered in the Palace Hotel as Mr. and Mrs. Tom White. They went upstairs to Room 203.

He found that the room smelled stale, like old socks, and opened the window to let in some fresh air. As he paused to look down at the dark street, she moved him over to see, too.

"I always wondered what it was like to look down on things from upstairs."

Both of them looked down at the street below, and he hugged her waist and smiled at her. "We should have a nice couple of days here. Then we'll have a tough week or so to get to the mountains."

She nodded, and when they straightened up, she put her hand up to clutch his neck. "I have already risked my life to get to El Paso."

He bent over and swept her up to kiss her. Soon they were in the bed, entwined in each other's bare arms and bodies, seeking the great explosion that came at the end. Mouths open, sucking in air for depleted lungs. Hips aching and pressing hard again and again to become one. His turgid shaft swollen painfully tight, seeking relief from such painful pleasure. Him over the top of her making the bed ropes creak under them in the wild flood of pinpoint needs—then at last he came, squeezing out an explosion of seminal fluid. He half fainted in spent exhaustion.

At mid-morning they all met at the livery and checked over the animals and equipment. Buck and Dyke were their usual hungover selves—grouchy as sore-toed bears. Slocum ignored them. He replaced two cinches that threatened to fray. Made some short leads that could be caught and used in case the mules need to be contained.

Using a chain twitch to each mule's nose to contain him, Slocum examined their hooves, and even rasped down some that had grown too long. He found no major problems, save for some stitching required on a few raveling saddle blankets. Doña did most of that kind of work. Slocum promised them that he planned to leave the next day at sunup and that anyone not ready would be left behind. At noontime, he and Doña washed up and left the others to go to find some lunch.

They had lunch with a street vendor who wrapped pulled pork, frijoles, and peppers in a large flour tortilla that she cooked on a small grill. She charged them twenty cents, and smiled at Slocum's extra dime. With their backs to a building front while they ate their noon meal, they could watch the trains switching and the yard activity that went on non-stop over the many tracks and sidings. Deming was a major hub for the Southern Pacific.

"All those trains that went whistling by me at that jacal either came from here or went here," she said. "I finally am seeing their source."

"Busy town. It use to be a wilder place when it was the hub for the track laying west of here."

"I bet it was."

From under the brim of his hat, Slocum watched a couple drive past in a buggy. He recognized Cindy Haller—he didn't know the well-dressed gent on the seat beside her using the reins on the spanking team of bays. He'd not seen her in five years. Obviously, she'd moved up in this world since he'd spent a fall helping her round up what was left of her late husband's cattle. Bennett Haller had been shot in a card-game brawl in Maricopa Wells during a layover there waiting for the next stage. Slocum felt somewhat obligated though he'd had no part in the shoot-out—he'd merely met the man on their ride between Tucson and Maricopa.

After being shot, Haller lingered a day or so. Slocum stayed around to see how it turned out. Before he died, he asked Slocum to take what little money he had left to his wife up in Yavapai County and help her sell the ranch and cattle so she could go back to Texas and her own people.

Busy chewing on his tasteful meal, he recalled the large mole he'd felt high up on the inside of Cindy's right thigh each time his hand slid in and sought her. He'd've known that gal anywhere.

"Siesta?" Doña asked, breaking into his memories.

"We better have one." He grinned down at her. This trip hadn't been all hard work. There was a little sunshine in the form of Dona. He wasn't certain what he'd have to do in those mountains down there to depose Durango, but somewhere between here and the Madres he'd have to devise a plan.

.

7

So many things on his mind. A school to reopen, and the guard that ran away last night. The one who had fallen asleep had deserted. Maybe someone let him out of the shed. It was supposed to be locked on the outside. What was his name? That ungrateful whelp. Durango should have left him in prison.

Besides, it looked like rain. The tall clouds that usually gathered and spread a few thundershowers every afternoon somewhere in the Madres already looked angry in the early morning. They were boiling taller by the minute as he studied them. Such storms caused flooding and mud slides in the mountains that made many problems for the villagers in the valleys. He shook his head and went back inside for a mug of pulque and to decide what he should do.

"Captain? Captain? We found his tracks. Contreras rode a burro for the east pass."

"Send some men after him," Durango said to Tomas. "I want that son of a bitch coyote brought back here."

"*Sí*, Captain."

"I have a job for the others. Tell every man they must come clean up the school. I want the walls plastered inside and out. The roof fixed so it don't leak on the children. I want some tables and benches for the students."

"*Sí*, Captain."

Durango put his boots up on the keg and leaned back in the chair. Tomas would get the job done. He'd gotten those washerwomen to come back to the river. Each day they grew braver and came closer for him to observe. Being the mayor was not so bad. He paid for the supplies the village needed from his huge treasury. Two large trunks of new coins, fresh from the mint, and stolen by his own hands.

There was Señora Valdez and her school—ah, the one who flowed like a willow tree in a small breeze, and his Marisel, the dark-eyed fawn. Both he wanted in his bed. Where was Lupe? Maybe the mayor had come home from hiding. As much as that woman liked a dick in her, she had to have someone poking one in her or she'd have been back by this time.

Maybe he should send again for Marisel. She had not been to see him since the day he was called away for that encounter when the rebels had murdered his Yaqui tracker and gotten away. He would miss not having Snake. Maybe he should find another tracker. If Slocum ever came, he'd need one.

"José?" he called to the bartender. "I need a good tracker."

The man came to the open door. "What do you need him for?"

"To track down my enemies."

"A man in the village called Santiago is one who can track."

"Do I know him?" Durango asked over his shoulder.

"You don't know him very well. He don't drink, Captain."

"Invite him to see me." Must be something wrong with a man that don't drink.

He raised the mug of pulque and with it he saluted the distant women doing their wash in the river. *To women and what's between their legs.*

He took a siesta, and woke from sleeping hard. Sitting up, he threw his bare legs over the side of the bed, yawning and blinking to get his eyes accustomed to the shafts of too bright sunshine coming inside his open doorway.

On his bare feet, he stood, wearing only a shirt, and stretched. The air of the room sought the exposed lower half of his body. Jolted by the realization that someone else was in the room, he dropped his arms and whirled around. Where was his gun?

Marisel was snickering at him. "I am sorry. I didn't want to wake you."

He grabbed for his britches and hastily put them on with his back to her.

"I only wanted to let you sleep." She came over and held his arm.

"I wasn't expecting you, I guess." He threw an arm around her and kissed her.

On her toes, she paused and looked him in the eye. "You weren't expecting me?"

"I hoped you would come. Only minutes ago I wondered where you were at." He combed his curly black hair back with his fingers and scratched the back of his head with both hands as he appraised her.

"Good, I want you to remember me."

He hugged her to his belly. "Oh, little one, I can't forget you—"

In minutes, he was kissing her on his rumpled bed. His hand was under her skirt caressing her silky legs. The dream would come true. He could see the fog over her eyes as he worked his hand to the junction of her legs and combed through the pubic hair. Easing them apart was no problem. She seemed totally under his spell. Soon, his fingertip penetrated her, and he smiled to himself over his accomplishment as he was busy tasting her mouth.

Caught in the wave of excitement, he quickly shed his pants and kicked them off his ankles.

"Should I undress?" she asked.

"Sure. Sure." He raised up on his knees to sit back and watch her undo the skirt.

She quickly shed it. He nodded, and she took the top off, and her perfect apple-sized breasts looked like ripe ones to him, so he ate on them. Both he and Marisel were out of wind, and his finger went in for one joint.

"It won't hurt me?" she asked, hugging herself to him.

"Maybe a little the first time. I will go easy."

He eased himself over her and put the head of his dick in the lips. Pushing against the restraint, he felt things give some and she sucked in her breath. More of an opening parted for his stiff cock as he increased the pressure to push it in. Her fingernails dug into his arms—damn, she was tight.

Then he drove his dick through her ring. She gave a small cry and he began to ply his dick in her. Under him, she was swinging her head from side to side. Then he came, and drew himself out. She would be great fun, he realized.

He was on his knees as she held her hand to her crotch and grimaced. "That hurt me."

"It will get better. That is what it was made for."

"Oh, it hurts. It burns like fire down there." And she clasped herself with both hands and curled up in to a ball on the bed.

"It will stop, I promise."

"Oh, it hurts bad."

He went to a trunk and found a bottle of laudanum and a spoon. "Take some of this, it will help."

"What is it?"

"Medicine."

He gave her a spoonful of laudanum and she made a face taking it. In a short while, her pain would be no more. He lay back down and cuddled her, feeling her tight hard breasts.

Kissing the back of her neck, he explored her body as

she became more and more relaxed. She reached back and pulled on his dick.

"You need some more?" he asked close by her ear.

"Sure, sure." She barely managed to talk.

He wet his lips and rolled her over on her back. On his knees between her limp legs, he pushed his pecker in her and she groaned. Thunder began to roll. By the time he was really going like fire and in her almost all the way, lightning struck a pine on the slope above the cantina. He thought he'd been hit in the ass when the sharp report struck his ears, and he came.

Exhausted, he lay on his back beside Marisel who had fainted, as the driving rain drummed on the roof. Icy air blew in the open doors and windows, so he got up and dressed, covering her with a blanket.

He wondered where the rebels would be hiding during this outburst. Usually, such storms were over in ten minutes, but this was a strong summer thunderstorm. Water began to find leaks in his roof, and the water all around the cantina was several inches deep already. It was coming down in buckets. He left the room and went into the cantina. It was crowded with wet men all in awe of this severe storm.

"Bad rain, no?" one of his men asked him over the mug he was ready to sip from.

"Raining hard," Durango agreed, and leaned over to take the mug José brought him.

"We could do nothing at that school," one of his men explained. And the others agreed. "It was raining too hard."

Durango listened to the nearby thunder as the lightning flashed and illuminated the entire barroom. He wondered if it would ever stop. Enough rain had already fallen as far as he was concerned, but there was no letup.

Soaked to the skin, Tomas came in. "The river is rising fast," he said.

Durango agreed. Rivers always rise when there is rain.

"I had to swim my horse to cross the ford," his man said.

A frown formed on Durango's face—already he'd had to swim the stream? Were they all going to be washed away? The cantina was fairly high above the usual river, but high might not be enough.

He walked over to Tomas and spoke above the storm's roar. "Tell the boy to take the horses to higher ground."

"Where? Up on the mountain?" Tomas looked at him in the dim light like he was crazy. "He couldn't get those horses in this weather to go anywhere. We might swim them across the river if we hurry. It is coming up fast."

"Juan, go see how much it has come up." Durango took charge. "Tomas, you and the others get the horses ready. We must get across the river and on higher ground." Pale-faced, José went with the others. It was something Durango would never have thought he'd do—abandon his cantina.

More lightning and thunder followed during the torrential downpour. In the room, he tried to wake Marisel. She was passed out. He took her limp form wrapped in a blanket and joined the last of his men as they pushed to the corrals. Water ran down his face and filled his boots. A burst of lightning blinded him for seconds as he bore his small load.

She moaned, as if inconvenienced by the whole thing.

"Shut up, you bitch. We must leave here now. I know you are wet and cold, but the damn rain won't stop."

When he was at last mounted on Eagle with her in his arms, he headed for the river. As he booted the hesitant horse into the water, he could hear the others trying to ride some horses and drive the rest.

"If we lose our seat, cling to me," he said to Marisel.

Her reply was to cling to his neck harder. Eagle soon was swimming, and the notion sent a bolt of fear up Durango's spine. He knew full well the only reason the big horse was swimming was because his feet no longer touched bottom, and despite his powerful dog-paddling, they were fast being swept downstream.

The damn heavy silver saddle—he should never have taken it. They rode waves like those in the ocean with her in his arms. Rain blinded him. Eagle soon breasted the current to try to get upstream and by the lightning strikes that exposed some landmarks, he discovered they were headed for the yawning canyon and the big rapids.

He tried to rein the horse toward the shore, but since he was holding Marisel as well, it was not easy. Eagle did a complete turnaround in the river despite his efforts, and that upset Durango more. Without spurs to control Eagle, he was worried that the headstrong horse might carry them to their deaths.

"We're going to die," she cried.

"No, we aren't. Stop saying that."

What could he do? How could he ever— Then the stallion began to reach shallower water, and Durango felt its hooves strike gravel.

"We're going to be safe," he shouted over the thunder.

She scrambled up and hugged his neck. "Oh, oh, we are going to live."

Eagle stumbled once, then recovered, and Durango resumed breathing again.

They stopped at the first jacal and made themselves at home, horse and all. The roof leaked, but half of the room was dry and they were out of the driving rain. There was more thunder.

How many men and horses did he lose in this flood? Only time would tell—if this damn rain would only quit. He stood in the doorway soaked to the bone and watched the unceasing storm continue. This valley would wash away.

Marisel hugged his waist like she was attached to him. He wondered about Señora Valdez. Was she all right? A shiver of cold ran up his spine—what a damn mess.

8

The knock on his door made Slocum bolt up in bed. Hand on his pistol, he cocked the hammer back and swung his legs off the bed. "Yes?"

"Señor. It is me, Enrique. Señor Buck and Dyke sent me to find you. They are having trouble with some bad hombres."

"Bad hombres?" He was fighting on his pants.

"*Sí,* they said for you to come fast."

"Where are they?"

"In a cantina called the Black Stallion."

Bent over, he pulled on his first boot, trying to remember the saloon and figure out why they'd need him. "You better go back and watch our things. This may be a trick."

"Two men I trust are doing that. One is a cousin."

"Good thinking." He used the mule ears to pull on his other boot.

Doña was already wiggling into her skirt in the room's darkness. "Who would give them trouble?"

He shrugged and buttoned his shirt. "They could be drunk."

She nodded in the darkness, pulled the blouse over her head and settled it in place, then went for their hats as she

73

opened the door for some light. When his gun belt was buck-led and his hat was on, he nodded to Enrique, who was stand-ing in the light from the doorway. The youth looked very apprehensive.

"What's happening, pal?" Slocum locked the door after Doña came out, and they headed for the stairs.

"Buck and Dyke have been winning at cards. These men won't let them leave until they win their money back."

"How many are there?"

"Four."

"I ought to even it out then?"

Enrique smiled. "Señor Dyke sent word to me by a Mexican boy they needed you *muy pronto*."

Slocum's boot heels hit the boardwalk hard as he turned to speak to Doña. "You keep your head down and out of the way."

"*Sí.* You do the same."

"I will. Let me go in first, then you two can slip in un-less it looks like gunplay."

They agreed, and he pushed through the black batwing doors. His hat was tilted back on his head as a sign to Buck. He never wore it like that. He nodded to the red-faced bar-keep behind the bar.

The poker game was down to five players, including Dyke and Buck. Two hard cases standing at the bar seemed to Slocum to be somehow involved—maybe as backup. He went down to where they had their elbows on the bar and watched the players.

"Good game going on?" he asked, making a sign to the bartender that he wanted a beer.

"Going good enough," the lanky one said beside him.

Slocum slapped a dime down for his beer and took a sip. Then he set the mug down on the bar. "You two might ought to go out the back way."

The lanky one frowned at him. A hard look crossed his face like he was close to exploding.

"Yeah, the town marshal stopped me down the block asking about two fellas—" He looked them over. "Yeah, fits your descriptions. He's working the places coming this way. Be here pretty soon."

"Obliged, mister," the lanky one said, and they cut out for the back hall.

"Where in hell're they going?" the fancy-dressed man seated at the card table asked.

He turned in his chair, and Slocum recognized him from earlier—the dandy husband from the surrey.

"I just asked if they were wanted by the law," Slocum said, and showed him his palms.

"Who in the hell are you?"

"Everyone hold tight." Slocum held his open hands out, ready to use them for whatever was needed. "The odds have just changed in here. Professor, you had enough poker?"

"I sure have." Dyke began to stand up.

"I told you that you ain't leaving till I get my fair chances to win that back." The fancy man started to rise and indicated the pile of money before Dyke.

"Mister—coming and going in a poker game is a man's private business," Slocum said.

"You better mind your own gawddamn business."

"I am. He's with me. And you can't draw that damn derringer up your sleeve before I can plant you in the ground."

The man sat down in his chair. "I never caught your name."

"Slocum's mine. Yours?"

"Martin Hanson—Texas."

"Nice to meet you. Buck, you two ready to leave?"

"Yeah. I was wondering what took you so long," Buck said, scooping up money and stuffing it inside his shirt.

"Hell, I figured only five of them, you could handle it."

"It was them two at the bar I worried about."

"They were wanted elsewhere," Slocum said. The other two men in the game looked a little pale under the skin.

Slocum felt Hanson was the main threat along with the hard cases at the bar.

"What's your business?" Hanson asked.

"Ain't got one right now."

"Hmm, much money as them two took from us, you won't have to work."

Slocum saw Enrique and Doña standing by the door. His palms felt wet—those two hard cases might double back when they saw no sign of the marshal. He kept an eye on Hanson, who never moved or turned. Slocum nodded good night to the tense-faced bartender and exited through the batwing doors, which squeaked when they swung shut.

Out in the night, he hustled the others down the boardwalk and dried his palms on his pants. "Those two might still be around if they figure I ran a bluff on them."

"Yeah, I could have handled Hanson and them other two, but the two you sent on bothered me," Buck said.

"Them sons a bitches at the start went to nicking cards with their fingernails. So me and Buck went to nicking them, too, until they were so confused and we went to winning." Dyke laughed aloud. "Served them right."

They came in sight of the livery and Slocum eased some. "Doña and I are going back for a little sleep. We're still pulling out at sunrise."

"Thanks. Good night. See you then," came from the three men as Slocum and Doña headed for the hotel.

"What are you thinking?" Doña asked.

"Today I saw that man in the card game with a woman I knew in the past. I'm just wondering why she's with that tinhorn."

"Women can make some poor choices, too," she said.

"Oh, yes?"

"I risked my life because I was so worried about my virginity being taken from me." She shook her head and looked at the stars for help. "One night I overheard the men I was going to El Paso with all say they planned to rape me. So I left them and walked miles on foot. To save my virtue, no?"

"I savvy that."

"Well, I get to El Paso and meet Antonio. He says he wants to marry me. He is so handsome—I never had a boyfriend before and he is so sweet. We make love—he wants to marry me. I am so excited. We make love. We do it all night and all day. Oh, I think I am so lucky to find him, huh?"

"Sounds like a fairy tale."

"It was. He gets me a little drunk, then he says he needs a favor. His boss where he works has a problem. And if I help him, he will get a raise and become the foreman. I am afraid but being drunk, I am finally convinced—for him— for him I will do this."

Slocum stopped on the hotel porch and hugged her. "So?"

"This man came in the room and he is big. I am afraid if I don't do this, Antonio will be fired. He unbuttons his pants sitting beside me in the bed and puts my hand on it. I don't know what to do. He shows me how, then he forces my head down there to suck on it."

"Tough lesson."

"*Sí.* He makes me drink more and then he climbs on me. He was rough. Even drunk, it was not fun."

"Sounds bad."

"That was just the start. There were four more came after him that night. That son of bitch Antonio was a pimp. Later that night, he told me he'd kill me if I ran away."

"What did you do?"

"I ran away to Mesilla. Better to be dead than his slave. I worked there as a cook and then I became a maid for a rich family, but her husband trapped me in the pantry and he stuck his finger up in me, promising me lots of money."

"I knew I must quit that job, and I met a man who said he'd take me home to the Madres. I wanted to go home so bad. But instead of taking me home, he took me to that jacal and he worked the cattle. I soon decided he wasn't taking me back, and then you came by."

He opened the door for her and let her go into the lobby. "We only have a short time to sleep. It's two-thirty."

She hugged his arm going up the stairs. "Then let's use the bed while we have one instead of sleeping."

He glanced over at her as he unlocked the door. "Sounds wonderful."

It was predawn and the jackasses were braying in protest about being saddled for the trip. Their noisy honking filled the darkness, which was cut only by the brass candle lamp Doña held up for them to see by. Four of them were working on loading one stubborn mule. They had his upper lip twisted in the chain twitch to force him to stand still and not kick. They made short work of the process.

"Is Slocum here?" a woman's voice asked.

He looked around, and Doña indicated he should come over. Slocum excused himself and went toward the lamp.

"This woman asked for you."

"Cindy?"

"Yes. He said you were here." Cindy smiled. "Said you robbed him."

"He lied." She looked nice, nice as she looked in Prescott that day when he put her on the stage for Texas. They stepped aside to talk more.

"Your husband?"

"Worse than that. He's my brother. We act like we're married to save an extra hotel room. He's into something with two hard cases. He won't tell me."

"They're outlaws."

She agreed.

"You need some money to get away from him?"

She hesitated and then nodded.

"How much?"

Her hand shot out to stop him. He waved it off and went to the others.

"Dyke, loan me forty dollars."

He stopped and scratched his sideburns. "Need more?"

"Nope."

With a big grin, Dyke dug in his britches and came up with a handful of money. "Here's fifty."

"Good." Slocum took it and went back to Cindy.

"You didn't need to do that." She shook her head. "Sorry I had to ask you for it. Come by the family ranch at San Angelo. I'll pay you back."

He hugged and kissed her. She looked ready to cry. "I owe you again."

"Naw. Go on. I've got to help the others."

Doña winked at him as he turned away. He tossed the canvas sheet over the mule and thought about Cindy's mole as Dyke and Buck tied the cover down in a diamond hitch. Some small details about a woman sure stuck in a man's mind.

Enrique went into the pen for the next mule. They were over halfway through the job. And Slocum felt anxious to get going west. They should be at Tres Palmas by late evening. And then came the bad desert that separated them from the Madres.

When the mules were loaded and the lamp put in the case and packed on the kitchen mule, they left the livery and went down Main Street, with the bell mare trailing Slocum's dun and the honkers behind her.

"So you are one who lends women money?" Doña asked in a low voice from beside him on her short horse.

"You need some?"

"No. But you told me about her and I wondered if you'd asked her along."

"She wanted to go home to Texas, not cross this godforsaken country with us to go fight some bandits."

"I bet if you'd asked her, she would have gone along."

He shook his head. Then he looked back in the soft light. Dyke, Enrique, and Buck had the mules in line. They acted much less shocked by the whistles and air brakes hissing from the tracks across the stream that morning. But Slocum had no regrets leaving Deming when they were out in the broad high plains and riding southwest.

Ahead of them, the Gambel's quail scurried off in the low scrubs and bunchgrass. Their whit-woo calls matched the doves that scratched in the dusty wagon tracks for bits of grain that had been passed through horses and dumped on the roadway.

The snap of a dove's wing taking flight made an unforgettable sound. There were plenty in this country. Slocum's dun set into a running walk. He intended to make the forty-some miles to Tres Palmas before sundown.

Cindy should be on a train for Texas by now. What was Durango up to? That was the bigger question.

9

Durango watched whole cottonwood trees being swept downstream past him and Marisel. If one of the trees had hit them and the horse, they'd have been swept under and drowned. The damn rain never stopped. Never let up. Lightning still blazed across the sky and thunder rumbled like a wagonload of potatoes.

This bitch of a storm had to stop sometime. But when? He wanted to raise his fist and threaten it, but that would do little good. He realized then that Marisel clung to his waist like she still had the same fear they'd shared crossing the swollen river.

"It is all right now," he said.

"I'm still shaking inside."

"You'll be fine. We are safe. We must get on my horse and see about the others."

Woodenly, she agreed with a nod.

He mounted his horse and jerked her up by the arm to sit behind him. Then he nudged Eagle toward the north hoping the others had gotten out upstream. He and Marisel had to cross a roaring side creek, and she screamed and clutched him when they entered the waist-deep water. On the high ground again, they began to find wet horses and sodden men in the continuing rain. The men struggled in the slick mud while leading their charges. There was no sign of Tomas. Durango kept moving north up the valley, crossing more engorged side streams that were bursting into the river.

At last he was past the spot across the river from the cantina. He could not see the cantina for the downpour, but recognized the nearby treetops that were half-swallowed by the raging flood. Satisfied that Tomas was not in that area, he headed up the road for a place to dry out.

He didn't want to stop at Señora Valdez's with Marisel behind him. The señora might not understand his hunger and need for women. With a smile on his lips under the sodden sombrero, he thought about having Señora Valdez. That would be a great victory for him—like a huge trophy deer head he could put on his wall.

He rode up to a jacal he knew was past the señora's place. A thickset woman came to the door and peered out, looking suspiciously at them.

"I am sorry, Señora, but we are wet and wish to share your casa."

"Come in, come in," she said as more thunder rolled over them.

Throwing his wet boot over the horn, he slid off the saddle. On the ground, he jerked Marisel off the horse. "We can dry out here."

Numbly, she nodded. He shoved her toward the woman's doorway. His boots squished when he stepped inside as the drumming on his hat quit. Then he stood there to let the water run off him in one spot. Marisel did the same.

"Come," the woman said to her. "I have clothes for you."

She led Marisel into the other room, and the women chattered in there. Soon, the woman appeared with Marisel, who was dressed in a white nightshirt that came almost to her knees. She was drying her short hair.

"You wish to dry, too?" the woman asked him as more thunder grumbled outside.

"Sure."

"I have some dry towels, but you will need to wear a blanket." She laughed. "I have no clothes to fit you."

"Fine," he said above the raging storm, and went in the other room to pull off his wet clothing. His boots would be ruined when they dried. He sat on a crate and pulled them off with a rush of water. Then the woman brought him some towels and said he could have the blanket off the pallet. And she left.

"Why don't you find me clothes?" he yelled after her. Undressed and under the woven cotton blanket, he brought out his clothing to hang up to dry.

As he entered the room, she looked up from building a small fire and mumbled, "I have no clothes your size."

Then she began arranging the wet clothing to get some of the heat. He sat on a straight-back chair and realized the drumming on the roof had stopped—the thunder was more distant. He got up and looked outside. The rain had stopped. There was a hush on the land—in the distance he could hear the roaring flood, but the noise and wind of the pelting rain had moved on.

He crossed himself and thanked God. Not because he was religious, or even because he feared the wrath of God, but it felt like the thing to do. Where was his man, Tomas? Durango would need a new second in command if the flood had washed Tomas away.

A rider came up the sloppy road and reined into the yard at the sight of Durango's stallion. "Captain. Captain. There are rebels up the valley. We got the word and Tomas sent me to find you."

Wrapped in the blanket, Durango went outside barefooted to speak to the man. "Tell him to bring the men and arms. We may have them trapped." His man was alive—good. The flood might not have cost Durango so much.

"You must stay here," he said to Marisel.

"I will follow you. Don't worry."

He hesitated, then shrugged. "Come if you must."

"Go," she said to him. "Don't worry about me."

"I must dress," he said, and the woman nodded, going outside so he could dress in her house.

His clothes were still wet, but he had no time to wait for them to dry. If he could break the spine of these fighters—then being mayor would not be so bad. He must make a good example of them. *You are Durango's enemy. You will feel the steel on your throat when he catches you.*

His wet boots were hard to pull on. At last, he stomped around in them to make them fit. Marisel held out his gun belt to him. He nodded. His mind was rolling over all he must do. He had to get those worthless coyotes who opposed his rule and end their lives.

With his his gun strapped on, he bent over and kissed her roughly, taking his soggy sombrero.

He left on the run, undid the reins, and used the horn to swing up in the saddle. Sitting upright, he waved to the two women and rode off to meet his men.

Hatless and in his muddy clothes, Tomas was directing the men when Durango came into view. Tomas rode over to meet him.

"We lose any men?" Durango asked, reining up.

"No, Captain. But we can't find two horses."

"They may show up. Where are these treacherous bastards?"

"We have word they are up the valley at a jacal."

"Let's ride and get them."

"*Sí,* Captain." Tomas shouted orders to mount up and ran for his horse.

They thundered up the muddy road with Durango in the lead. The sun was out and the temperature was going up as they loped their animals—an armed force on serious business.

When the jacal came in sight, Durango slid the gray to a halt and held up his hand. His men formed a line. Some wore sombreros, others were bareheaded, and many balanced rifles on their legs. They looked to Durango to be a formidable force as he twisted in the saddle to look them over.

Ahead, he saw a few of the resisters hurry for the jacal. Durango divided his forces and told them to dismount and have the boys hold the horses. He instructed the men to surround the jacal before anyone fired a shot.

"I will shoot the first shot," he said.

They gave a cheer and spread out as instructed. He dismounted and gave the reins to a boy. Then he set out for a cottonwood log to use it for a shield. Three others ran behind and to the side of him. A bullet tore his sombrero off his head. The bullets were like hornets. But they reached the large log and once behind it, he loaded the rifle's chamber and on his knees, swung up to take aim, using the log for cover, and emptied his rifle into the front door.

Rifles and pistols spoke in a chorus of shots and black smoke that silenced the shots from inside. Wounded men were crying and others cussing from the jacal.

"Surrender," he ordered.

A volley of shots answered him. Two bullets tore bark off the log, but he remained unharmed. His men poured more shots into the jacal that raised adobe dust and a fog of black smoke that the soft wind moved away.

Only the sounds and complaints of the wounded in the building could be heard as silence fell.

"Surrender," he demanded.

"What are your terms?" someone inside shouted.

"Terms? I have no terms. Surrender or die are my terms."

"Wait—"

"I won't wait long." He wiped his palms on his nearly dry pants, anxious to have this over with. Then, from the smoky doorway, they came out, hands high. Some were bleeding and wounded. Others, mere boys, showed the fear on their faces.

"Go see about the ones inside," Durango said to Tomas.

Then he turned to his prisoners. "Hold your hands behind your heads."

He set the rifle down, stepped across the log, and walked toward the eight rebels, confident that he had the lot of them.

"Where is this Sanchez?"

No one answered.

"Is he here?" he shouted at a boy on the edge of the group.

"No—no, Señor. He is not here."

"Valdez? Is he here?"

"No, Señor."

"Captain. There is one dead and two wounded in here," Tomas said from the doorway.

Filled with rage, Durango looked hard at his man. "Why are they all not dead in there?"

"*Sí*, Captain." Tomas drew his knife and went back inside. The screams of the wounded were soon cut off, and he reappeared wiping the blood off on his pants.

Birds sung in the cottonwoods. Wind rustled the leaves. One of Durango's men brought a chair out of the jacal for him to sit on. In the warm sun, he looked over his prisoners. They were a scruffy lot now that they were captured. How could such a mangy bunch have caused him so much lost sleep?

"How many more of you are there?"

No answer.

He crossed his legs and interlaced his fingers. "I will start killing you one at a time until I have their names. Your chance to live is simply tell me the names of all my enemies in this village."

No one spoke.

"Take that one over there." He pointed out the boy who had answered him.

Reyes took him by the collar and removed him off to

the side. He forced the boy on his knees with his head bowed down.

"Do you wish to die?" Durango asked.

"Nooo."

"Tell me what their names are."

"I—I can't."

"Is your memory so bad you are going to die for it?"

"Madre de Dios. . . ." The boy began to pray and sob.

Durango waited until all he did was sob. "Shoot him."

Some of the other prisoners started to rise, but were put down by the rifles of Durango's men. Reyes cocked the pistol with a loud click.

"All of you are wasting my time," Durango said. "Get two out there."

"Durango?" A man of thirty stood up. His shirt was bloody from a wound as he faced the outlaw leader.

"What do you want to tell me?"

"That boy Francisco is only twelve. He came to see his brother. He knows nothing of us."

Arms folded, Durango considered the one on his knees under Reyes's muzzle.

"Then you will go in his place?"

"Yes."

Durango turned his head to the side to look at this one. "Are you his father?"

"No."

"Then why do you do such a thing?"

"Because he is just a boy who does not deserve to die. He does not know our names nor has he turned a hand against you."

"But he is here."

"He only came to see an older brother who he missed."

"Shoot him instead," Durango said, and recrossed his legs. A man like that could lead an army against him. Better he was dead. Durango would be glad when he was dead.

So, as the day wore on, they shot all of them. No one gave a name. Then only the boy was left, and Durango had Tomas bring the boy up to speak to him. Holding him by the scuff of his neck, Tomas dragged him forward until he was only a few feet away from Durango.

"Who was that man who saved your life?" Durango asked.

Out of the boy's dark eyes, raging hatred glared at Durango. He spit in Durango's face.

The spittle ran down his cheek. This little bastard had spit upon him, never flinching, never ducking away from the punishment he expected to receive. He was no innocent child—he was one of those that lay about dead on the ground. A soldier.

" 'Cut his damn throat. He is one of the lice here."

Tomas obeyed, and Durango wiped the spittle on his sleeve. It required two tries to get it all off. When the boy's crumpled body was at his boots, Durango ordered his men to line up the bodies in a row so their families could claim them.

The outlaws moved aside to the cottonwood trees, and someone found two goats recently butchered. Durango told them to cook them and they'd have a feast. Tomas sent men for some wine and other food. He hoped they weren't some of Señora Valdez's goats.

Seated on a horse blanket in the shade, he observed the mourning families finding their men or sons among the dead. A priest came and gave last rites to them. Durango drank some brandy from a bottle one of his soldiers gave him. He didn't care for it, but he drank it anyway.

Marisel came and stood before him. "Are they all dead?" she asked.

"*Sí.*"

She drew a deep breath and then forced a smile. "I want to sit on you."

"Sure." He patted his legs.

Boldly, she raised her skirt so her bare butt would be on his legs, straddled him, and then lowered herself on his lap. With a small smile of mischief on her mouth, she wiggled so he knew her crack was riding over his right leg.

Then she moved closer and hugged him. He savored the moment. *You little bitch, I'll show you—*

Somehow she jerked out his .45, cocked it, stuck it in her mouth, and fired it. His ears were pierced by two needles from the blast and he fell over backward, and she spilled off his lap.

Pushing her away, he scrambled to his feet. Blood poured out into the hair on the top of her head. Her eyes were blank in death's arms. In disbelief, he stared at her lying there, the smoking pistol beside her hand.

"Why in the fuck did she do that?" he demanded.

Tomas stood beside him, looking at her, and shook his head. "I have no idea."

His skull still rang inside like a massive bell. Gun smoke burned his nose and his sinuses. His stomach roiled. That stupid bitch!

10

Agua Primera meant First Water.

They crossed through a land of curled-up pancake pads, black-edged as even they died the slow death of drought. Bare brittle thorny plants loomed in the sandy waves, and heat waves distorted the horizon. The wind-sifted dust over the tracks of the so-called road obscured their way. Mummified dead horses and cow carcasses were strewn alongside the road, with even the scavengers' own bones littering the ground. Some bones were covered with bits of long-dried hard skin—some with hair on them.

A hot sun broiled the land. Vultures circled overhead with patience.

"Eerie damn things, ain't they?" Dyke asked, removing his hat to wipe his face on his sleeve.

"Yeah," Buck said. "I had one shit on me once, and had to throw away my hat and shirt. You couldn't get it out."

"Why did they do that?"

"They were eating on some folks killed in an Injun raid. Pissed me off so bad that when I found 'em, I ran up there shooting at them. They all took off, and one shit on me getting away."

"Don't shoot any today," Dyke said.

"If I do, I'll be sure they crap on you."

"Ah, damn you, you're just jealous of my hat."

"Why, I wouldn't wear that thing to a cockfight."

"You'd be the height of style wearing it. Slocum, are we making this Agua Primera place tonight?"

"We should have no problem doing that," Slocum said. They'd made good time so far. He had no worries about them arriving there late that afternoon or early that evening. The mules and horses were fresh enough to hold a jog and cover lots of ground. But he'd not have to rock any of them to sleep that night.

"Tell me, Doña, is Agua Primera a fine metropolis?" Dyke asked.

"No." She laughed. "It is a dried-up place like the rest of this country."

"Oh, what a shame," Dyke moaned. "I was expecting the amenities of civilization."

"Not there." She shook her head under the wide-brimmed sombrero. She turned to Slocum beside her. "This was the place where I quit the party I was with and went on my own. I think they planned to sell me as a slave when they got through with me."

"You were lucky to survive."

She agreed. "But I might not have lived if I hadn't left."

"Yes, you're right."

"Besides, I'd've never met you and Dyke and Buck." She turned in the saddle to smile at them.

"Doña, I am certain that you could have done better than us."

"Oh, Dyke, you three are gentlemen and travel in class."

"I guess we'd beat riding a burro across through here. Slocum, you ever been through here before?" Dyke asked.

He held up two fingers. "Once with a company of U.S. troopers and once with a shipment of ore from a mine."

"Why bring ore out this way?" Dyke asked.

"Because of Old Man Clanton. He was preying on such

shipments. Besides, we were bringing in bullion under that ore and needed to avoid the check stations." Slocum twisted in the saddle to look the train over.

"I guarded a couple of ore shipments," Buck said. "Brought them out through Naco."

"You ever tangle with Clanton?" Dyke asked.

"No. I had seven Apache scouts hired and they had new Winchesters. The old man didn't want to tangle with them."

Slocum nodded. "I bet he didn't."

The sun had set, and darkness enclosed the country. Stars had begun to shed pearl light over the land. Slocum thought he could see a light ahead. The mules were doing lots of weary snorting, and so were their horses. Five or ten miles more.

The starlight soon made the road apparent, and he could see the light ahead every once in a while. At last, they topped a rise and the small cluster of buildings and corrals could be seen.

"Keep your wits about you, folks. Many of these places are run by outlaws. Doña, can you shoot a gun?"

"Sure."

"I have a .32 Colt. It's small enough to fit your hand." He handed her the holster set from his saddlebags.

She stood up in the stirrups and strapped it on.

"Fit?" he asked.

"Last hole." She laughed, showing him the long tongue. Removing the small revolver, she hefted it in her hand.

"It has five shots in it. Don't shoot us," Slocum said with a laugh.

"Oh, no, don't shoot us," Dyke said.

Slocum reined up and made the others stay out at the edge of the settlement while he rode in. The mules braying would have brought out anyone—a bearded man came on the porch, leaned on the porch post, and whittled.

"Evening," Slocum said.

"Yeah, how many head?"

"Five horses and eleven mules."

The man looked out in the night and whittled on his stick. "People?"

"Five."

"Cost ya eight bucks to water them and use the corral."

"Kind of high, ain't you?"

The man laughed. "You can ride on."

No need in arguing when you couldn't win. Slocum stepped down, dug the money out, and paid him. He went back to the dun and started to mount.

"You been here before?"

He stopped to listen to the man. "Yes."

"I thought I knew ya."

"Name's Slocum."

"Yeah. If them mules out there bust down my pens, you'll pay to fix it."

Slocum nodded. Two more hard cases came to the lighted door and looked him over. Maybe they needed work rebuilding the pens. He'd post guards all night—this bunch wasn't a Sunday school class. More like pirates at sea. He swung up in the saddle and gave them a grim nod.

"Well?" Dyke asked him when he joined the others. "What's the word?"

"Water them and feed them. We ain't unsaddling them."

"Huh?" Buck asked.

Slocum lowered his voice for the four of them. "I wouldn't stay here tonight, but our animals need the rest and they'll need a drink before they start out in the morning."

They agreed.

"I'm like Doña was, I don't trust them." Slocum shook his head. "All in my guts, but I trust it."

Buck nodded. "We better set up shifts to guard."

"We can do that," Slocum agreed.

Enrique shook his head. "*Malos hombres*. I only paid him a peso to water my horse the day I got here, and I rode right on. They are not good men."

"Eat, feed them, and go to sleep. I'll wake you up if I need you."

When the animals were crunching their hard corn noisily, Slocum carried his Winchester while scouting around the pens. The hard cases would probably wait until they thought Slocum and his friends were asleep, then sneak up. Such good mules were valuable, along with the equipment—and lives weren't worth ten cents around men like the hard cases here.

Mules snored and stomped in their sleep. A desert owl hooted and a coyote howled in the night. The Big Dipper turned like a clock on the mantel keeping time for Slocum. While he was squatting with his back to the fence close to two a.m. in the morning, by his calculation, Doña came and joined him.

"Anything?"

"No."

Then some glass bottles rattled over near the main building and someone cursed. A hiss silenced his foul mouth.

"Wake Buck and then Dyke, but smother their mouths. They're coming."

She agreed.

"The boy, too."

Slocum went over the fence and crouched low. The Winchester was in his hands.

"Where're they sleeping?" a voice asked.

"Hell, probably in the open—"

Slocum was looking down his gun barrel at a third man. "Hands high or die!" he shouted.

"You son of a bitch!"

The rifle barked red fire. The bullet staggered the man and he crumpled to the ground. The next cartridge in the chamber took down another of them, and the last man ran away.

Slocum reloaded his rifle. Then, cocked and ready, he

was on the move. He kicked the first man's handgun away. Then he bent down and took the other one's pistol, jamming it in his belt. They were both shot through the torso. He hoped they owned funeral suits.

"Who's left?" Buck asked him.

"One more ran off."

"Where did he go?" Buck asked Slocum as they were joined by Dyke and the others.

"The main building. Enrique, you and Doña watch the mules and horses. We can handle this." Slocum waved for the other two to spread out

The mules were awake, milling and braying from the gunshots. It would be hard to hear anything with all that going on. No lights were on in the building. The small porch was dark with shadows. Best Slocum could figure, the last man had run inside to hide.

"You don't want to be burned out, then come out," Slocum ordered.

"*No! No!*" a woman shouted. "Don't burn my casa."

"Send him out."

"How can I?"

"Lady, you better talk him into coming out or I'm torching the place." Slocum knew she was standing close to the door, but he couldn't see her. He signaled for Buck to take the back door. Buck left in a jog.

"I can pay you," the woman said.

"We want him out here. He aimed to rob and kill us."

"But I can't make him."

"He'll come out when the fire gets hot enough."

"All right. All right," a man's voice said. "I'm coming out. Don't shoot."

"No tricks."

Someone appeared, hatless, hands high.

"Get on the ground facedown, spread-eagle."

"Huh?"

"I said facedown on the ground now!"

He went to his knees and obeyed.

"Watch him, Dyke."

There was a struggle going on inside. Slocum had made it to the doorway when he heard Buck swear. "Damn you, lady. You don't want to be busted over the head with this shotgun. Get to going."

Slocum caught her by the back of the neck and hauled her outside. "You aimed to shoot us, huh?"

"No. No. I only wanted to protect my house."

"Sit your butt down." He forced her down on the dirt.

"She was trying to load it when I slipped in the room."

"I'd say we're lucky we ain't buzzards' bait."

Dyke leaned his butt against the building and sighed. "They not only don't have amenities, they don't have good manners."

"What do we do with 'em?" Buck asked.

"Tie them both to the fence. Feed and water our mules and horses again. Then we'll get the hell out of here."

"What about the other two?" Buck asked.

"Would they have buried you?" Slocum asked.

"I doubt it."

"I doubt I'd worry about them then."

Buck agreed.

"Let's feed the mules and get the hell out of here," Dyke said as they herded the pair to the corral. "This is some kinda hellhole."

The two were tied spread-eagle on the corral rails. Slocum collected all their guns, holsters, and ammo and put them in a pannier. They might need them later. The others fed the stock.

He found some cheap whiskey in the main building and set two bottles out. That plus the shotgun and shells would make an armload.

"What do you need me to do?" Doña asked, bursting into the room.

"Take these two bottles, wrap them in some towels so

they don't break, and pack them. We may need to have a drink later on sometime."

"You have not slept all night."

"I'll be fine. We're alive anyway."

She hugged him. "Someday you will ride away and I will cry. Did the rich widow who gave you the mules cry when you left her?"

"I imagine so."

She nodded. "You have no wife, no home?"

"A long time ago a young man got drunk. He'd lost heavy in a card game and he came back to kill me. Needless to say, I had to shoot him. His grandfather owned the law, judge and sheriff. He keeps two Kansas deputies on my trail." He shook his head and looked off at the bright stars.

"Where will you go when this is over, back to the rich lady?"

"In my life there is no going back."

"But you could stay in Mexico."

"No. There are greedy men down here, too, who want to collect bounties."

"I will miss you, too."

"Hell, girl, I'm not gone yet."

She shrugged. "Maybe I need to drink this whiskey."

He shook his head. "That wouldn't cure a thing."

They were still days from the mountains, but two more days of hard pushing and they'd be in the foothills. Cooler, more water, and better people—he hoped. And maybe an answer on how to dislodge Durango.

11

By late afternoon the water had gone down like it came up. They crossed to the cantina in the belly-deep stream. Obviously, the floodwater had never gotten too deep in the building. His bed was dry, though there were signs the water had come through his room several inches deep.

He took a mug of pulque and dropped in his chair outside. The river had scoured much of the land between him and the water's edge. The two lost horses looked beaten up from their experience. They'd stood hip-shot at the corral when he'd ridden in. *That crazy little bitch.* He was still puzzled by her suicide. He planned to forget her. The vision of what she did made his stomach churn.

What would happen next? Being mayor was hard work. If he didn't have the money from the mint robbery, how could he have run this place? Maybe that was why no one had ever taken over this valley. It was too poor to bother with. There were no cash crops. Corn to make his beer had to be brought in. Barely enough food was raised to feed everyone. The men of the valley used to go off to work and bring the cash back to live on. Only by financing this whole business could Durango even stay there. Now Señora Valdez wanted a school fixed up. More money. He shook his head.

How did officials ever raise money? Taxes. But you couldn't get taxes out of this place. Still, he liked the lifestyle, and the government would never try to stop him. Who would care about such a place? Bandits all over Mexico held small villages like this under their control. It was good to be here— floods or no floods.

An hour later, riding a burro sideways, Señora Valdez approached the stream, which was higher than usual. He saw her coming. She dismounted, then led the burro down to the edge of the water. Then she mounted again, like she had a sidesaddle, and rode across. Such a lady. In his life he'd known many *putas*, sluts, and other women who were common as grass, and none had matched her gracious ways. Truly a princess.

"Ah, Señora Valdez." He stood in the doorway, his right arm on the hand-hewed frame, and studied her coming up the pathway.

"Good day, Durango. How are you?"

"I am drying out."

She looked around. "Yes, I guess we all are. I am fortunate. My place was high enough to miss most of the flooding."

"What can I do for you today?"

"I wondered now the rain has passed us if we can resume work on the school."

"In the morning?"

"That would be fine."

"In the morning I will send some of my men to help you." She nodded.

"Would you have a glass of wine with me?"

"If that is your wish."

"Wish? That is an order from the mayor." He laughed and then went to the side door. "Wine for the lady and pulque for me."

When he came back, he discovered she had chosen a chair outside under the grape vines, and he joined her on a chair opposite her. This was a game of cat and mouse. But it entertained him.

"How much schooling do you have?" she asked.

He made a zero with his thumb and forefinger. "There was no time for school in my life. My mother and I had to work all the time just to eat."

"Then how did you learn this business of leading men?"

"You don't need to go to school to know that, Señora." He leaned back in the chair. "You ever watch a pack of dogs?"

"I'm listening."

"The toughest one whips all the rest in line. Number two whips all the rest except the leader, and so on down the line. You don't need to go to school to know that."

"So you are the alpha?"

"I don't know that word."

"Alpha means A and that means first."

He settled in the chair. He even liked how she talked about things. Alpha meant number one. Then Tomas was B. A, B, C, that was all the alphabet he knew. Who was C? He'd think on that.

"See, if you could read, you would know how great men like Napoleon thought."

He narrowed his eyes at her. "I would know what was in their minds?"

"Yes. Reading books can do that."

He looked across the silver stream. Sunlight danced like diamonds on the water. If he could read, he would know what such men thought. There would be power in that. But he was not a boy to go back and make a mark on a slate board and recite lessons.

"Do you have such books?" he asked

"Some."

"Would you read them to me?"

"I could read some of them to you."

Good, maybe he would learn something from that. "Thank you, Señora."

"I will read to you after the school is fixed and when I have a teacher to instruct the children."

"A teacher. Where is there another teacher?"

"Two women in the village were taught in a convent and one man studied for the priesthood. They can teach, too."

"Good. Let's get the school fixed. I want to hear about Napoleon."

She finished her wine and thanked him. Then she left him, took her burro to the water's edge, hopped on it sideways, and rode across the river. He watched her while sipping his pulque and wondering what she would be like in his bed. Where was her man?

Valdez and this Sanchez were the two keys to the resistance. If he ever found them, his days after that would be spent with pretty naked maidens feeding him grapes. Or he'd have a torrid session in his bed every day with Señora Valdez.

That night he could hardly sleep. He tossed and turned. In the middle of the night, he could see no light coming from under the door to the cantina. It was late. On the edge of the bed, he mopped his face in his calloused hands. He should go and check on his guards in the morning. Were they ready to send up signal fires?

That would give him plenty of time to do what must be done. He might not be able to read, but he understood war. He would check the pass in the east in the morning.

At dawn, he had the boy saddle Eagle, and instructed Tomas to finish the school to suit Señora Valdez in two days. Then he rode upstream to check on things in the eastern pass.

Birds were singing and the sun was bright. He felt dull-headed and kept trying to shake it. He had not had strong coffee that morning. Then his stomach began to roil and cramps set in. Bent over in the saddle, he rode a ways and decided that maybe if he stopped and emptied his bowels, he'd feel better. No one lived around this area, so he decided the willows would be the perfect place to do that.

He dismounted, hung his sombrero and gun belt on the saddle horn, and went in to the willows over his head to find some relief. He pulled his pants down and squatted, and the growing wind swept his bare butt. Gas and diarrhea exploded, and he was cringing at the pain when his world went black for a second. Then he was facedown in the dirt and some madman was smashing him on the head with a rock.

Screaming and cursing at him, Durango tried to roll away from his attacker. Willows blocked Durango's way, and he was attempting to kick his pants past his boots. In a fury, his soles struck the man with the great rock and sent him backward into the willows.

You son of bitch. It was Umberto Contreras, the escaped one. Durango used his hands to rip loose his britches. Where was his knife? Contreras roared like a lion and charged him. The rock was so big that it made the man clumsy and Durango avoided him, coming to his feet.

Durango reached over his shoulder and found the long-bladed knife in the sheath that was there under his weaved vest. Armed with the gleaming blade, he began to parry back and forth with the red-eyed, crazed Contreras. The willow stalks that Durango straddled tore at his privates when he moved, but he paid them no mind. They not only hindered his movements, but they also slowed the rock bearer. This was life or death for both of them.

Durango realized that if the man had chosen a rock half the size of the one he had, he himself would already be in Hell. Durango made several attempts to stab him, but Contreras used the flat stone for a shield. Making loud curses and grunts as he brandished his rock, he forced Durango backward. The men were evenly matched at the moment, except that the cramps in Durango's belly about doubled him over. This was no time to be sick. Had he been poisoned?

He backed up to get the man in the open. Durango could get to his horse and gun. Willow branches and leaves tore at him, but he couldn't protect himself while being attacked by a madman.

"I am going to hang your balls and pecker on a lance," Contreras threatened, then stepped back and held the stone up high.

Durango saw a chance to slice the man's fingers. But in his rush to do it Contreras managed to kick him in the crotch, then swung down with the rock. The pain was so great that Durango doubled over and the rock glanced off his head. Holding his aching privates in his left hand, he rolled over and slashed Contreras's leg.

The cut went deep in the calf and the man howled. He fell on his back with the stone on his chest, and Durango leaped on top and stabbed him in the neck. Contreras made gurgling sounds and blood soon frothed from his mouth. Time and again, Durango stabbed him, until he collapsed in exhaustion on top of the damn rock. Then his rear end began emitting gas and more hot fluids he could do nothing to stop.

"You son of a worthless bitch."

Dizzy-headed, he staggered to the stream and removed his boots. The water was damn cold, and he shivered washing himself off. His bowels cramped several times, but nothing came. Climbing up the bank on the sharp rocks to get out, he puked, then puked again.

What was wrong? The sourness was streaming out his nose, and he wanted to escape to somewhere where either his belly didn't double him over or his tongue didn't threaten to fly out.

Staggering around in the willows, he found his soiled pants. Shaking the once-white britches, he realized there was no way he could wear those crap-covered things back to Antonio. Holding his nose, he took them down to the stream and beat the soiled places with rocks until most of the fecal matter was gone. He hung them to dry. The poor washer-women, he thought as he straightened up and felt the sharp pain in his lower back. Soon, the pains in his guts forced him to squat again to defecate more hot fluid.

His britches finally dried and at first he felt too sick to pull them on, but he finally made the effort and then staggered to his horse, which was busy grazing. Lucky for him that damn Contreras hadn't gotten his gun off the saddle. That no-good sonabitch.

It was past sundown when he dropped dizzy-headed out of the saddle and stumbled in to flop on his bed. José soon came in to see about him. "Señor, are you all right?"

"No—have them put my horse up. I have been sick and had the shits all day."

"What can I get you?"

"Nothing. Leave me alone. I think I have been poisoned."

"Should I send for Tomas?"

"No. Let me die." Curled in a ball, he hugged his sore roiling belly and shut his eyes to the pain.

First that stupid little bitch Marisel shoots herself in his lap, then he gets attacked by that deserter, and to top it off, he'd been poisoned. What would happen to him next?

12

Cedars began to appear. Slocum and the others were climbing in altitude, and while the Madres had still not appeared, he knew the mountains would soon be seen on the horizon. It would be good to escape the desert. That evening they camped at a watering hole under some cottonwoods in a wash. They decided not to cook a meal, ate some peppery jerky, and Slocum assigned guard duty. He turned in, and hardly awoke when Doña joined him under the blanket. It might be hot as hell in the day. During the nighttime, the heat evaporated and a blanket felt good.

The others let him sleep, and when he awoke, it was near dawn. They were saddling the braying mules. Doña came over and squatted down with a cup of coffee for him. "We decided you needed to sleep. So we did the guarding."

He smelled the wood smoke and nodded. "Thanks, I did need it."

He sat up and blew on the steaming coffee. "I better go help them."

She shook her head. "They have everything handled."

"We should be close to the foothills if we aren't going the wrong way."

"No, I remember this place. Tonight we will be at Santo Tomas Mission."

"Small irrigated place, right?"

"It is a nice village. The people there were kind to me."

He pulled on his boots. "Good. I better go help the others."

"Food will be ready shortly."

"Sounds great." With his boots on, he rose to his knees and kissed her. "Sure glad you came along."

After her beans and tortillas, they rode out with the rising sun at their backs. At noon they climbed a rise, and the majesty of the peaks came into view as if they'd been made to appear by some witch's magic spell.

"Pretty sight," Dyke said. "I may never leave here. Is there any other way back?"

Slocum shook his head, then reconsidered. "Oh, you can ride up into Arizona and take a train back."

"A much more civilized way to travel."

Everyone laughed.

Irrigated plots began to appear: beans, corn, and alfalfa. Slocum gave Doña money to buy some roasting ears and green beans from a woman on her way to market with them loaded on a burro. Small ditches carried water to the fields, and killdeer chased the bugs roused up by the liquid. Doves sang in the cottonwoods, and the green crops were easy on Slocum's eyes after days of the sand's glare.

"It sure is heavenly here." Dyke said, riding his mule beside Slocum. "Not bad at all."

"We can rest here a day. Feed the animals some hay and check everything. Maybe someone here has some word on Durango and what's happening in the valley."

Dyke nodded. "We do approach the enemy, don't we?"

"He's still several days away. But yes, we do."

"It seems like we've been going there forever, and here we are at his doorstep."

Slocum nodded. His eyes narrowed at the sight of three

dusty men on horseback in the square wearing bandoliers of ammunition across their chest and rifles slung over their shoulders.

One of them was herding a pretty girl who carried a water jug. His white teeth flashed under the black beard. No matter which way she turned to escape him, he spurred the sweaty chestnut over to block her.

"Get Buck up here," he said to Doña under his breath.

With a nod to indicate that she understood the situation, she whirled the short horse around and raced it down the line for Buck.

When Slocum saw Buck coming for backup, he tossed Dyke the mare's lead. "Hold this for me."

Slocum sent the dun forward, sliding him on his heels to cut the man off, and wheeled the gelding around to face him. "Leave her alone. Can't you see she needs to get some water?"

Anger flashed in the man's dark eyes over someone interrupting his game. He checked his prancing horse. "Who are you, gringo?"

"Name's Slocum. But the game you play on her is not funny."

The man tapped his chest where the belts crossed. "My name is Muerte to you."

The other two who sat their horses laughed aloud at his words.

"You have a suit with you?" Slocum asked.

"What for, gringo?"

"Hell, they can bury you in those dirty clothes, I don't give a damn." He noted the girl had gone inside a doorway.

"You are telling me you are going to kill me over having a little fun? Huh, compadres?" he asked the others without turning.

"Rey, he don't know you are a fast gun," the one on the left said.

The other one laughed aloud. "Him and them two old men will make good buzzard bait."

Rey nodded, and had to check his horse, which was foaming at the silver spade bit's edges in the corners of its mouth. Bobbing its head and fired up, it half reared. With his gloved right hand, Rey smacked it on the head, but that only made the horse dance more in place.

"Gringo, get out of my way."

"Make me."

Anger flashed again in Rey's eyes. The horse darted to the left. Rey's right hand went for his gun and he was forced to check the horse with his left hand. Slocum's gun hand filled. The .44 bullet struck Rey in the chest. The frightened horse reared up over backward and the saddle horn stabbed Rey in the breastbone. He never moved after the horse rolled off him.

The rider on the left took a rifle slug from Dyke that peeled him in a cartwheel off his horse. The other rider broke for it, spurring his horse, and met the "old man's" fire. Buck shot him twice and the horse, pulled over by its stricken rider, spilled on its side.

Gun smoke and dust fogged the square. Doña rode over and took the dun's reins as Slocum dismounted. He kicked the gun from Rey's outstretched hand and walked over to check on the second man.

"Damn, these people are savages," Dyke said beside him with his smoking rifle.

Slocum looked around. Buck was shoving the third man's gun in his waistband and nodded—his man was gone. The second man, with a bloody hole in his chest, lay on his back in the dust and blinked up at Slocum.

"I wasn't going to die today—guess that won't work."

Slocum nodded. "Better make some peace with your Maker."

He shook his head. "Too late—"

And he expired.

"Señor. Señor?"

Slocum looked up.

"My name is Salvador Delores. I am the mayor. Thank God you came today. Oh, those men were bad outlaws and they have terrorized us for a long time. Come, all of you, into the cantina. We will buy you food and liquor and have a fandango."

Dyke licked his cracked lips and set the rifle on its butt. "Now there is a man of my own heart and mind. Did he say food, liquor, and a fandango? My, my, now ain't that something."

"After we water, feed, unload, secure our stuff, you can fandango for two days."

"Now that's going to be all right."

"I will get help. You can store your things in my store," Delores said.

"That's a start," Slocum said as they gathered the leads of the mules. Doña took all their horses to the water tank at the well.

People came into the square from everywhere. A boy got on the hand pump and worked it to keep the trough full. Two more took the reins and told Doña they could handle the horses. Some men came, took off their sombreros, and shook Slocum's hands in gratitude. Then they packed the bodies off to lay them in a row on the ground outside the church.

Panniers were carried inside and when everything was in the store, the men from the town begun taking off the pack-saddles and blankets. The packsaddles were set on their ends and the blankets draped over them to dry.

"Manuel has plenty of hay for them," Delores said. "We can take your animals there."

"I'll pay you," Slocum said.

The short man shook his head and indicated the dead men. "To be rid of them is worth feeding them all year, *mi amigo*."

Slocum clapped him on the shoulder. "*Muchas gracias*."

"A lady has offered me a bath at her house and some clean clothes to wear to the fandango," Doña said.

"Go," he said, and playfully slapped her ass. "See you later."

She rushed off. The horses and mules were led off to be corralled and fed. Delores joined Slocum, and they walked to the trough. Slocum handed the mayor his hat to hold, and dropped on his knees to dunk his head in the cool water.

It felt good on his sun-scalded face. A bath would be nice, but at the moment he didn't care. They were through the worst part of the trip.

"Tell me, what do you hear about Antonio?" Slocum asked.

"The bandit Durango has an army up there. It must be bad. All the time rumors of killings from up there come out. He had three children murdered because their father killed a man who was screwing his wife. Then Durango killed her. Cut her throat. He is a mad butcher."

"How many men does he have?"

"Many. I don't know. This Morales you killed here has been demanding many things from us. We have lived in terror here, Señor, for a long time."

"He won't bother you anymore."

"I am so glad for that. Come have a drink with us. The women will fix food and we will dance and sing all night to celebrate our freedom."

When they entered the cantina, the thumping music had already started and Dyke was stomping around the room with some ample-bodied woman who sounded pretty free. Her shrill voice was yipping like a coyote as he spun her around. At the end of their dance, he removed his hat and bowed to her in grand style.

Buck stood with his elbows hooked on the bar, drink in hand. He nodded and turned to the bar when Slocum joined him. "Ain't never a dull moment with you."

"Thanks," Slocum said, and nodded to the bartender, who was ready to pour him some whiskey. "Go ahead."

"Leave the bottle," the mayor said, and pulled Slocum over. "Does your compadre like women?"

Slocum turned and smiled at him, "He loves 'em."

"Huh?" Buck asked, not hearing it all.

"He wanted to know did you need a woman."

Buck leaned around Slocum and grinned at the mayor. *"Sí, señor."*

Delores waved the bartender over and whispered to him. The man nodded and took off.

"He's going to get you a real one," Delores said.

"Well, I'll be damned," Buck said, and downed his whiskey. He reached over and splashed some more in his glass. "Who is she?"

"Her name is Carmela. She is a widow," said Delores.

"Sounds interesting." Buck twirled the ends of his mustache and reset his hat on his head.

Carmela arrived, and it looked like she had been dragged from her cooking. She was busy smoothing her dress and fluffing her hair. She looked thirty, with a nice figure and smooth features. She made a smile when Delores introduced her.

The music was slow, and Buck took her hand and they danced away. Both of them looked into each other's eyes like they were starstruck. Slocum nodded his approval to the mayor. That would be fine.

The whiskey going down cut lots of trail dust in Slocum's throat, and in minutes he was dancing with a plump woman. Her name, he learned, was Estrella and she assured him that she could take care of him if he needed it.

"I will be ready," she said with a promising grin as he circled her around.

"What would Doña think?" he asked, amused by her openness.

"Oh, she can watch us do it," she said, and laughed

aloud. Then she shut her eyes and cringed, all red-faced, at her own words. Shaking her head, embarrassed over her outburst, she buried her face in his vest.

"Should I tell her that?" Slocum asked.

She looked up. "No, she might kill me. She didn't look a bit upset being in all that shooting."

"I don't think she had time to do much else."

Estrella agreed, and at the end of the music returned him to the bar. "We all appreciate what you did today. Those *bastardos* really belonged in Hell."

"Yes," Slocum said, nodded to her, and turned back to his drink.

Doña came through the doorway wearing a pretty blue skirt and blouse. A smile covered her face. "I borrowed this while my clothes dried."

He hugged and kissed her. "Good thing you got here. There's many single women here."

"I came as fast as I could. Who is in Buck's arms?"

"All I know is her name is Carmela. They went and got her for him. I think she was in on the cooking when they enlisted her."

"Pretty lady."

"And he ain't half bad as a dancer either."

"No, he's not. Have you heard about that murderer Durango cutting children's throats?"

She looked at him with a frown that hooded her brown eyes.

"I know, it's sickening," Slocum said.

"Sickening is not a good word for it."

"We'll move him out, either back to prison or feet first."

"I want to help you."

"You already help me."

"No, Enrique wants to go back to the valley and see what he can learn about things. I want to go, too."

Slocum shook his head. "I can't let you. Too dangerous.

You know no one. No. If it was your village, I'd say okay. But you don't know who you can trust in there."

"I am not a child."

He took her threatening fist into his own, and slipped away with her in a waltz. The crowd was growing and the revelry grew louder. Dyke and the high-breasted woman were still dancing.

"You're not even thinking about it, are you?" she demanded.

"I'm thinking I don't want to see you dead. This man's a rabid killer."

She hugged him. "I want to help you, understand?"

He moved her in small circles through the crowd. "Too damn dangerous."

"We'll see what's dangerous when we get into bed tonight."

Slocum pulled her closer, so he could feel her body against his. There would sure be a fight—but he knew when she made her mind up, Hell couldn't stop her.

What was that damn Durango doing?

13

The *bruja* brought him some tea made from blackberry roots. It didn't taste that good, but she promised it would stop the diarrhea. He wanted to fan his butt hole; it was so sore he couldn't sleep on his back or get a hard-on without it bringing him close to tears. He'd never considered giving women up before—but it had become a reality in his pain and discomfort. He no longer sat in his chair—he stood or lay on his belly.

So when someone said from the doorway that the señora was crossing the stream, he got off the bed and straightened his clothing. He went and stood under the grape arbor, watching her come up the flood-scoured slope. She could walk through a field of flowers and not crush one.

"I understand you've been ill," she said, looking at him hard.

"I am fine now."

"You look peaked."

"I don't know how that looks, but I am fine." He adjusted her chair and then went to put his forearm on a post of the arbor.

"You've lost weight and your color is sallow," she said.

What color was sallow? Hell, he'd have to agree with

117

her or she'd know he was stupid. All he could think about was feeling her long breasts and shoving his dick into her. The longer he thought about it, the harder his tool became.

"I really came to tell you next week we will have classes."

"How many children are going to be in the school?"

"That's why I came here. The people are not convinced this is a real school."

"Real school? What can I do?" What was wrong with them?

"Tell them to send their children."

A pain shot up his rectum and he gritted his teeth. There was no way he could even do it to her without screaming from the pain his actions would cause him. He forced a knot from behind his tongue. "I'll—I'll have Tomas do it. They will be there."

"*Gracias.* I can see you are in much discomfort today. I'll leave you. I hope you get well soon."

He nodded and let her start to leave. Then he called, "Your husband is still away working?"

She nodded like someone who had agreed to something simple.

He drew in a sharp breath. The pain ran up his spine. Son of a bitch, his own hard-on was killing him. He turned to his door to go inside. He must tell Tomas to get her some students. Damn that bitch anyway for making him that worked up just watching her hands flutter like butterflies on flowers. Damn, he hurt. At last he had his pants open, lying on his side in bed, jacking off until he finally came, and then he fainted and the iron hand crushing his ass let go.

The next morning, he began to worry if the medicine had made him constipated. It had been twelve hours since his bowels had made him cringe. Maybe he'd need dynamite to take a shit.

"Captain?" his man called to him.

Good, he would learn how many children Tomas had sent

to school. Rising, he closed his pants and went to stand in the doorway to talk to Tomas. "How many children are going to be there?"

"Twenty-seven, Captain."

"Good."

"Have you seen the mayor's wife Lupe lately?"

"You want me to invite her to come here?"

"No. No." Not at this time anyway. The notion made him want to stand on his toes to escape it.

"Do you want Lupe or the señora, Captain?"

"Neither one today." Lupe? Hmmm, his own man might be the one satisfying that horny bitch. If she wasn't getting it from somewhere, she'd already have been back to see *him* by now.

"By the way, I think someone is stealing some coins from us, Captain."

"What makes you think that?"

Tomas shrugged. "I see here and there some shiny coins being used in trade. We never paid our men with them."

"No, but we have paid for the pack trains of corn, the liquor, and the money for the flour and things needed at the store."

"But I think whoever is stealing them is paying *putas*. I will watch close and be sure. The locks are on the door and both trunks. He would have to be a good thief to steal from that."

"Yes. But I better not catch them stealing." They had some of the best crooks around in his gang. Durango would watch, too.

"Are you feeling better?" Tomas asked.

"All but my butt. It is sore and hurts."

"Did her medicine work?"

"Yes, it did. *Gracias*."

"They said she was very good."

There was a rider coming down the road. Durango stepped outside and combed his hair back. The young man was a stranger to him. He bounded off the horse and rushed up, looking very excited at both of them.

"Who is Durango?" the boy, who was in his late teens, asked.

"I am. Who are you?"

"Miguel Marietta. I use to live here with my Aunt Veronica. I work at the Palomino Mine. But I was in Palo Alto last night and a man told me that there was an army coming up here to run those *bandidos* off."

"An army?" Durango said too loud.

"*Sí. Sí.* There is an hombre named Slo-dum coming with an army of men to fight you."

"You mean Slocum?" He stared hard at the boy.

"That's his name. Yeah, that's it. Do you know him?"

"Yes, we know him. Was he there already at Palo Alto?"

"No, Señor, but he must be coming this way hard I was told."

"No mention of how many men he has?" Tomas asked.

The youth shook his head.

"Are you here to visit?" Durango asked.

"Yes, to see my aunt. She is like a *madre* to me."

"Thank you for the news. We will be ready for this *bandido* Slocum and his army. I owe you for this news."

"No, no. I love this valley and coming back here. I am glad my aunt is protected by you." The youth excused himself, bolted into the old saddle, and crossed the ford.

Slocum, that son of a bitch, was coming. Bringing an army, too. Durango began to pace back and forth under the grape arbor looking at his once-pretty boots. What would a general like Napoleon do about such an attack?

"We better warn Mateo," Tomas said.

"I have a plan."

"What is that?"

"All that blasting powder we got in that pack train robbery. We can set charges on that mountainside on the north side above where the trail is so narrow. Trap his men in there and blow it up."

"That would be how to handle a large number of men."

Durango looked across the stream at the washerwomen, thinking hard about this new problem. "We would need to set it up quickly. Get as many men as you can and go do that today. Tell Mateo to be on the lookout for any of Slocum's spies trying to come in."

"Yes, Captain."

In a few hours, they left for the east pass using horses, mules, and burros for pack animals. There was much braying, kicking, and cussing going on. But they soon formed a line and rode for the pass with men alongside on horseback whipping the laggard animals.

It would take them a day to get it done right. But when it was set, Durango could imagine an army buried under the rocks, gravel, dirt, and trees that would rain down on them. A perfect solution. He felt so much better later that afternoon that he ordered Nalda, the bar maid, to bring him enough hot water for a bath.

He had some clean clothes he had been saving. They were from a dead rich man, but he had no fears about wearing such things. The white shirt was made of silk and the pants cotton, but not hard-woven cotton such as most workingmen wore. If his butt kept improving, he might go and see Señora Valdez at the end of her school day. He had done her many favors—he was ready to collect on her debts to him.

Nalda brought the steaming water in wooden buckets, and he soon was in the copper tub soaking his sore butt. It felt good.

Slocum—he was coming with a damn army. That son of a coyote bitch.

14

Slocum held Doña tight in his arms—her firm body pressed hard against him. He didn't want to let her go. Enrique stood close by in the night holding their horses' reins.

"I know we need to know what they have planned down there. But promise me to take no chances. Both of you. They are vicious killers. Him and his henchman Tomas."

"I will learn all we can," Enrique said. "But if we all go into Palo Alto together, someone will see we are with you."

"We'll be there tomorrow night," Slocum said, knowing the young man was right. There were spies all over who for ten centavos would tell Durango anything. "You two be careful going into the valley. Is there anyone to hide you there?"

"Yes, there will be some of the resisters to hide us. One man's name is Carlos Sanchez, the other Burt Valdez, who is a smart man. He's an engineer for the mines. We will be careful passing through Palo Alto not to be seen."

Slocum nodded. He'd heard those men's names. He tossed Doña on the horse, then clapped her leg. "Take good care of yourself."

She planted a kiss on his forehead and she and Enrique rushed off in the night. Slocum had bad feelings about them going into the valley, but he needed information on the size of Durango's force and the arrangements, if any, to fortify the place.

They all missed Enrique and Doña the next morning when they had to pack out with no hot breakfast to eat. Dyke grumbled all day about letting their cook get away.

"I'll buy your dinner in Palo Alto," Slocum said finally to shut him up.

"I want a beefsteak cut off a fat steer that's the size of a saddle blanket and slow-cooked over a mesquite fire."

"Probably be oak," Slocum said over his shoulder. "This high up."

"And maybe a woman with big tits to serve it like the one back there," Buck said.

"Was her name Rosita?" Dyke said, riding in to spank a lagging mule with the tail of his rope.

"Damned if I know, but she sure had a set of 'em. Wasn't there a redhead up here at Palo Alto last time we were here?" Buck asked.

Slocum nodded. "Angelita was her name."

"Tell you what, Dyke. There are some damn pretty women in these mountains."

The mules went to braying, and Slocum saw a rider coming off the mountain though the pines on a short-coupled mountain horse. The pony had a great swinging walk. It was a deep-colored sorrel with a blazed face. The rider was a straight-backed man who had been to cav school, because he rode square-shouldered.

He stopped his horse on the flat and waited for them. Then he rode over and shook Slocum's hand. "Burt Valdez. Glad you are here."

"Slocum's my name. Enrique said you'd be around the area."

"Is he with you?" The man looked around the train for him.

Slocum shook his head. Something made him cautious. Valdez might be all right, but Slocum wasn't telling him everything until he knew him better—in Mexico men could be on one side one day, another the next.

Slocum finally spoke. "He's to meet us in a few days."

"There are more men coming?" Valdez asked, looking shaken.

Slocum shook his head. "Buck, Dyke, and me. And Enrique."

"But the word was that you had an army of men."

"Whoever said that must have been cross-eyed and counting double."

"These men are killers. We have lost over a dozen men to their treachery. They have even murdered three small children and a woman and raped many more. It will be hard to fight against so many."

"We've heard part of it. How many men does Durango have?" Slocum asked, letting the animals breathe in the thin mountain air.

"Maybe two dozen. All well armed. All cutthroat killers from the prison."

"Unless we can enlist some more men up here or out of the valley, then we must divide and conquer them."

As if in defeat, Valdez dropped his chin. "We have failed at that so far. The men left in the village are too afraid to raise a hand to help us. I can't blame them. So many of their good friends have died a bloody death."

"I understand what you are saying. Meet Dyke and Buck," Slocum said.

Valdez rode over and shook their hands. "*Gracias.* I am sorry, but I am so concerned about this matter and so far all of our plans have failed."

"Let's talk and ride," Slocum said, anxious to get the animals put up and settled in. They were still several miles from the village.

"What can I say?" said Valdez. "They pardoned Durango, I'm told. Maybe his mother found the money. The word is he had some money stashed from past robberies and she used it.

Then he got his henchman Tomas out the following month. He kept buying pardons until he had enough men to take over the valley. They have guards in this east pass and some in the south."

"How many?"

"Three or four at each one. They won't let you in. They'll shoot you unless you have a pack train of supplies."

Slocum twisted and looked back over his train. That might be an idea.

"The man in charge of the east pass slips into Palo Alto and has an affair with another man's wife. But we saw no reason to capture him up till now."

"Now there may be a reason. Durango must have a way of being warned."

"Oh, I never thought about that. A way to signal him that trouble was coming, right?" Valdez reined his horse around a large boulder that split the trail.

"Exactly. Will this woman cooperate with you?" Slocum twisted in the saddle to wait for his reply.

"That I don't know. But we can capture him away from his post."

"Good first step."

Valdez shook his head. "I've met a few men in my life that would have scoffed at such odds as we face and acted much like you do. I see perhaps why you were able to take him to the *federales* last time."

"Buck back there gets half the credit."

Valdez turned in the saddle and nodded at Buck. "I guess I expected a hundred mercenaries."

Slocum laughed. "These horses, mules, and supplies were all charity. Hell, man, where would we have gotten the money for mercenaries?"

"I'm not sure. I guess I listened to too much gossip."

"Some great general said divide and conquer. I've used that philosophy for years and it will work. Where can we store these supplies and put up the animals?"

"The Palomino Mine. I do some engineering work for the manager and he will see nothing happens to anything."

"Is it close to the village?"

"Yes."

"Good. I promised those two a good supper. They missed breakfast this morning."

"What would they like?"

"Beefsteaks, large size."

"That can be arranged."

"Now you're talking," Dyke shouted. "Big ones."

Late in the afternoon, they rolled into the Palomino Mine's pens. The mine was well guarded and Slocum could see there was lots of security there. Dave Burton, the mine manager, welcomed them and assigned some men to help them unpack.

Being an American, he had many questions to ask them about what was happening at home. He was a New Yorker who after so many years of working in Mexico had lost some of his accent.

"Of course I have no proof—they must have murdered my packers and dumped their bodies—but I believe this Durango stole an entire pack train of blasting powder, caps, and sticks. Some of my mules were later found by officials in Juarez. The man who had them claimed he caught them running loose."

"Durango has a long record of being a bandit. Thanks for putting our animals and goods up. We should not be long," Slocum said.

"Take as long as you need. I want Durango gone from these mountains."

"We'll try to make it quick."

They hiked with Valdez back to the village. Slocum noted that the man appeared as comfortable walking as he did riding. His new associate seemed to be a real outstanding person. Slocum even felt niggled that he didn't have an army of mercenaries with him.

This village, like so many of these small clusters in the Madres, was on a stream with a wooden bridge to join the two sides. Slocum could see from the dried trash that a flood had recently been through there. "You had some rain?"

"Big rain. Too much, too fast. It drowned many people." Valdez shook his head.

"I saw the high-water marks on this bridge."

A short climb up the steep road, and Valdez sent them to a cantina while he went to find the meat he'd promised them. The bartender, Benito, apologized that his liquor supplier, who came up through the valley, had not delivered anything to him in weeks, but said he did have red wine.

Slocum ordered a gallon of it, and the three took seats around a table on the patio as the sun edged downward. It felt good to be off his horse. But he still felt like he was in the saddle. Where were Doña and Enrique?

Valdez returned with the meat and said Benito was a good chef. He delivered it to the man, and came back out to join them.

Half standing, Slocum poured him a glass of wine. "How else can you get in the valley since they have the roads guarded?"

"Oh, if you're half goat you can take a dim footpath down into the canyon. The rain and flood trapped some of our men in there and he slaughtered them." Valdez shook his head in disapproval. "Once we used a windlass and got some men in and out on the south end, but it was too dangerous. We did send them back a Yaqui killer named Snake—dead in the cage."

"Slocum and I couldn't find him when we rounded up Durango the last time," Buck said. "He was dangerous as any rattler and earned that name."

"Yes, and he was Durango's tracker. No man could match him either."

Good, that meant there was one less of the tough ones,

thought Slocum. He toasted the others with his goblet. "To Durango's demise."

A young boy came and stood by Valdez. He whispered something in his ear. Valdez nodded and paid him ten centavos.

"*Muchas gracias,*" the boy said, looking delighted at his reward.

When he was gone, Valdez leaned forward. "We have plenty of time to eat. He just told me that our man is in the house. Her husband is gone and that means he usually stays the whole night."

Slocum nodded. "Eat hearty, guys, we may have some work to do."

Valdez agreed.

Full of beef and beans, they set out in the shadows of a night of stars and barking dogs. When the house was surrounded, Slocum and Valdez eased to the open front door. The jacal was dark, but the sounds were obviously of two people actively engaged in sex, with grunting and groaning and the slapping of skin on skin. Their guns drawn, the two men went inside, Slocum in the lead. He could make out the two people on the pallet and stepped over to clunk the man hard on the head with the butt of his pistol—he went down like a poled steer on top of the woman.

She began to scream, but Valdez was on his knees beside her; he covered her mouth. "Shut up or your husband will know all about this."

That worked. Slocum dragged the limp man off her. The man began to moan. Slocum shoved the pants off the floor in his face. "Put them on and be quick."

"Who in the fuck are you?" He sat on his butt, shoving his feet in the pants.

"The man who is going to rack your ass."

"All right. All right. Did her husband hire you?"

Seated with her back to the wall, the woman let out a small scream at his words, hugging a blanket to hide her nakedness.

"That's for me to know and you to find out," Slocum said, shoving the shirt at him. "Now get up. I ain't got much patience, so move."

"All right. All right."

"Remember," Valdez said to the woman, shaking his finger in her face. "If you speak one word of this, your husband will know the whole story."

She crossed herself, and held up her hands clasped together. "I swear to God I will tell no one."

"Good. See that you don't," Valdez said.

They hustled the barefooted Mateo through the starlit night and into a nearby shed, and sat him down in a high-back chair for interrogation. A candle was lit and put on the table, and Buck tied Mateo's hands behind his back and to the chair.

"We want to know everything about the guards in the pass," Slocum said.

Mateo spit on the table.

"That wasn't smart," Slocum said. "I can jerk your toenails out one at a time, then start on your fingernails. You'll want to talk when I get through with you."

"Fuck you."

Slocum caught him by the shirtfront with his left hand, and slapped his face back and forth with his right hand. "I'm going to clean your talking up, too. You savvy?"

"All right." Blinking his eyes, Mateo tried to look around and see all of them. "Then you kill me?"

"It depends," Valdez said with his arms folded over his chest.

"Depends on what?"

"Did you kill any of our men in the canyon?"

Mateo shook his head. "I stay at the pass all the time. And if you give me a horse, some food, and a canteen, I'll ride so fast from here it will spin your head around. Wait, wait, I'll tell you all his signals and what he planned for you hombres."

"The straight of it?" Slocum said.

"Every damn detail."

Valdez looked at the others. Buck nodded and so did Dyke and Slocum.

"Start at the beginning," Valdez said. "You lie to us and we'll cut your throat. Tell us the truth, you can ride."

Mateo nodded. "There are three other men at the pass. They are very lazy and it will be easy to jump them without me there."

He looked around in the flickering light for their nods before he continued. "A bunch of his men were up there a day ago setting charges on the mountain so when this army of Slocum's gets past the guards, they will blow it up and bury them."

"The guards were going to let them in?" Slocum asked.

"That's his plan. One man at the gate, the others hide, and they set off the blasting powder when Slocum and his men are in the canyon."

"Did he steal that from the Palomino Mine pack train?" Valdez asked.

"I wasn't with him if he did. There are two stacks of fire-wood up on the peak. One's got lots of boughs in it—it will smoke. The other one will smoke less but make a helluva fire."

"How were you to use them?" Slocum asked.

"Use the smoky one for the daytime to say that Slocum's army is coming. The dry wood at night so they can see the blaze."

"How many total men does he have?" Slocum asked.

"Four up here. Three, I guess, at the south pass." Mateo shrugged. "Three, maybe four been killed. Two more just ran off, his man Tomas told me, when they were setting the charges. He only had about twenty counting him when we came up here."

"He's down to a dozen," Dyke said. "I thought he had an army down there."

"Don't get too confident," Slocum said. "They don't wear uniforms so you can't separate them from the others."

"Right. I understand that, but still, it isn't like fighting fifty of them."

"He's got ammo and guns," said Mateo.

"Rifles?" Slocum asked.

"New ones, Winchesters, and enough ammo to fight an army."

"Where's he keep them?" Slocum asked

"He has this bunker. I think it was once built to be a burial vault. It has an ironbound door with a big brass lock. I don't know what he has in there. Lots of loot he brought in by pack train when we first got here."

"Where's this bunker at?"

"You go up the canyon behind the cantina. It's high and dry up on the left hillside. You can't miss it."

"Anything else we need to know?" Slocum asked. He knew about the old vault, but he'd wanted to test the man's accuracy.

Mateo shook his head. "I got out of prison thinking I was going to heaven up here. I swore I never was going back to jail. When I saw some of them little girls being raped, I knew I had to get out of there. So I took this post and he thinks I'm loyal to him."

"I'll have a horse, saddle, and some food for you in an hour," Valdez said. "If you circle back or warn him, I will personally cut your head off and mount it on a pike."

Mateo swallowed and nodded that he understood. "Could I send a note to Lola and ask her if she would come with me?"

"Does she have a horse?"

"*Sí, señor.*"

"Can she even read?" Slocum asked.

"I don't know."

"You stay here. I'll go ask her."

"Gracias."

Slocum paused. "She might say no."

"I understand. Tell her I love her."

With a nod, Slocum turned to the others. "Untie him. I'll be back with her or her answer in a little while."

In a few minutes, he was at her dark doorway. "Lola?"

"Who is there? Go away." She sobbed.

"Come to the door and talk to me."

"Who are you?"

"That's not important. Mateo has a horse, some food, and wishes for you to leave here with him."

"You are a liar. You only want me to come out so you can rape me."

"If I'd wanted to do that, would I have called you out here? No. I'd've rushed in there and done it."

"Who are you anyway?" She wrapped the blanket tighter around her.

"Tonight I am your friend. He must leave here in an hour. He said to tell you he loves you. He feared that you could not read his note."

"Good thing." She threw the blanket up to make a hood over her head against the growing night's chill, then rewrapped herself. "I can't read."

"What shall I tell him?"

She nodded. "Tell him I am coming. I must saddle a horse and get a few things."

"Where is the horse?"

"In the corral. The saddle and all is there."

"I'll get it. You get your things. Time is short."

"Yes." She looked to the stars and crossed herself.

She had some pouches ready to tie on behind the saddle when he led the mountain horse up to her door. When they were all on the horse, along with a blanket roll, she took the reins. "How far is he?"

"A short ways."

"I will walk there."

"Fine."

"What is your name?"

"Slocum."

She nodded in recognition. "He said you were coming with an army to take back the valley."

"To free the people."

She slapped at her dress with the reins. "And me."

"You?"

"From another dictator—my husband."

In the starlight and the light of the quarter moon, he could see a saddled horse outside the silhouette of the shed. "Oh, I see they have his horse here already."

She caught Slocum's sleeve. "Wait. I have no way to repay you. May I kiss you?"

He swept her up and kissed her, then set her down. "God be with you both."

Her eyes twinkled even in the dim light. "He will be, Slocum. *Gracias.*"

The soles of his boots made a gritty sound along with the plodding of her horse. Where were Doña and Enrique? He hoped they were safe.

A mountain loaded with blasting powder waited to bury him. He needed to quickly end Durango's reign of terror. She hugged Slocum, and then she and her horse ran on ahead into the night.

Good-bye, Lola. Good-bye.

15

Durango rode the stallion across the stream and around some debris left from the flood. Birds sang and the day was bright. Cottonwood leaves rustled over his head. Doves dusted in the road and cracked their wings taking off at his approach. It was a good day to be alive.

He glanced toward the pass high above and to the east. The trap was set. *Come on, Slocum—I will bury your ass and all your mercenaries with you. Ha—this time I will prevail.* Tomas had come back from supervising the men setting the charges so they would work.

Mateo, his man up there, was strange—he never took a day off. He never came down to drink or screw some of the women. Maybe he went to Palo Alto. Tomas said he was the best man for the job. He really made the others stay awake on guard duty and do it right. No one came by that post that he didn't question. The other men, they just complained about having to work a few days.

It was so much trouble. Durango yearned for a large ranch, a hacienda, a beautiful woman in his bed, and many cattle. Then he could be with real rich people, people who acted like she did—Señora Valdez. He would have to learn to stop scratching his nuts in public, but he could do that.

What did rich people do when their balls needed scratching? Endure it, he guessed. They must be tough not to ever fart in public or belch out loud. Damn, it would be real rough trying to be rich. Drink tea in little cups. Hell, he could drain one of them in one swallow. Maybe he would be rich and not be part of their society. Unless his fancy wife dragged him to their events.

At last, he was at the schoolhouse. And could hear the children singing inside the school. My, they sounded sweet. He dismounted heavily. His silver spurs clinked like small bells. She came to the doorway as the children went right on singing. She crossed to where he was hitching his horse under a gnarled tree.

"Señor Durango, I want you to do something about Felix Arroya."

He smiled and took her in, much like a man took in a pile of pure gold ore. "What is wrong, Señora?"

"Last night he raped one of my students."

"How old is she?"

"Did you hear me?"

"I hear you fine. How old is she?"

"Eight."

"Oh, that is bad."

"Bad?" She drew a deep breath. "That is disgusting and he must be mad."

"Probably just horny."

"Horny!" She threw her hands in the air. "No, you know what he is?"

"What?" He had expected her to start hitting him.

"He's an animal. You stop him or I will stop him, and I'll cut his balls out and feed them to him." Her last words were said through clenched teeth.

He held his plams up. "I will see what I can do."

"Do!"

"Sí, sí, I will see what I can do about him."

"Then do it right now." She pointed toward the road. "I mean now."

He unhitched his horse. When she was mad she was really mad, and maybe could beat the hell out of most men. He didn't want to fight her, he wanted to make love to her. "I'll go see about him."

"If you don't—"

"I know. I know what you will do to him." Taking hold of the saddle, he swung up, dragging his chaps over the gray's rump. "I will be back."

"Bring his *huevos* back, too."

He wanted to ask if she would nail them on the classroom wall, but she was already so mad she would find no humor in that. "I will see you later," he said.

With a wave for her, he rode out in a lope. He knew where to find Arroya. The man lived in a jacal up the valley with a woman who had several children. It might have been one of her daughters he'd nailed. Durango kept the horse on the run the entire way, and pulled him down when they approached the small farm.

Eagle started dancing on his front hooves as Durango let the stallion show off coming up the lane. A woman hanging clothes to dry on a line looked at him fearfully. She began to run for the jacal's front door, but he cut her off with Eagle and stepped down to grab for her arm.

"Was it your daughter he raped last night?"

Her face went stone white and she nodded woodenly.

He shook her. "Why did you let him do it?"

With a look of bewilderment, she shook her head. Her copper lips were pursed tight.

"Next time, hit him over the head. I won't have this happening again. You hear me?"

She fell at his feet in a pile and began sobbing. "Nothing I could do."

"Nothing, my ass. Is he in there?"

She nodded quickly.

He went to the door and saw the hump of the man's body under a blanket. Fiery mad, he went over and kicked Arroya hard in the kidneys. But it was not like kicking a live person. And Arroya never woke up from the blow either. Durango turned him over. Arroya was dead.

He looked up. The woman stood in the doorway with both hands clenching a rag to her mouth, awaiting his rage.

"You killed him?"

"Y-yes. I had to."

She'd shot a mad dog. Maybe not shot him, but at least killed him—Arroya was damn sure dead.

"I don't know your name."

"Marta."

"Marta, I will send the men and a wagon for him. His funeral will be at sundown."

"*Sí, gracias, patrón.* I will have him ready."

Durango nodded in acceptance. For a moment, he considered stepping down, slicing off Arroya's privates, and delivering them to Señora Valdez. Then he changed his mind—she would think of him as vulgar. Maybe he was.

At the school, he dismounted and Señora Valdez came outside.

"He won't do it again."

She frowned and blinked her eyes at him in disbelief. "You mean you shot him?"

"No," he said, slapping the reins on his chaps. "Her mother killed him."

"I see."

He nodded and swung up in the saddle again. Seated, he straightened. "So how is school?"

"Doing very well. Very well. Thanks to you."

"Call me when you have any problems."

She agreed and he rode off. Once again she had escaped his clutches. *Damn her anyway.*

16

Slocum stood on the porch of the cantina. He planned to give Enrique and Doña a couple of days. Maybe if they stole the guards' horses so they couldn't leave the pass, the guards would not tell anyone about Mateo's desertion. If Durango thought that Mateo's desertion was part of a plot to storm the pass, he might fortify it.

Earlier, Slocum had seen two Apaches squatted in the sun near the small store. They had to be renegades—up here the people had a live-and-let-live attitude. The Apaches came and went in many villages that showed little hostility toward them. Merchants found the red men had money from raids, even gold, which the Indians valued only for things the yellow iron would buy.

"*Yut-a-hey,*" he said to them in greeting, and squatted down.

They nodded.

"Would you steal some horses today?"

Both of them peered hard at him. Their coal-like eyes watched him with narrowed lids like one did a buzzing rattler.

"You *tonto loco*?"

"No, I will pay you to steal them."

The older held out his calloused palm.

Slocum put a dollar in it.

The man smiled.

"We need more money." The other one elbowed his buddy aside.

"You steal them today from guards in the pass. I'll pay ten pesos." He held up his fingers to show them how many.

"What we do with them?"

"Eat them. I don't want the horses. I want the horses gone today."

"Today?"

"*Sí.*"

"Ten pesos?"

"If you hurry."

"Where you be?" the older one asked.

"Cantina."

The two took off in a trot.

Slocum smiled after them. Those horses would be gone within the hour. He climbed the rock steps to the cantina and found Buck and Dyke at a table drinking wine.

"Well, what now?" Dyke asked. "All they have is this grape piss to drink."

"The guards at the pass will shortly lose their horses."

"How's that?"

"The finest horse thieves in the world were sitting around, and I hired them to steal the horses. They get to keep them and I pay them eleven dollars for stealing 'em."

Both men laughed.

"I seen them yesterday," Buck said. "Just sitting around."

"What's for breakfast, besides wine?"

"Benito will cook you some eggs and some sausage."

"I better get him to do it." Slocum twisted around in his chair to look for him.

"Ah, Señor, you are ready to eat?" the bartender asked, coming outside on the shady veranda.

"I'll have the eggs and sausage."

"Scrambled?"

"That'll be fine." Slocum leaned back in the chair. "I'll take coffee, too, if you have it."

"*Sí.*"

"Anyone seen Valdez since we sent Mateo and his girl-friend off last night?"

"No," Buck said. "She say much when you went and got her?"

"Said she was escaping a dictator, too."

Both men nodded their heads.

"Women get tired of that slave business in a hurry," Dyke said.

Valdez had not shown up when the Apaches, yipping like coyotes, rode up to the foot of the stairs with five horses.

"Guess they want their money." Buck began laughing. "Damn good wages."

"I don't mind paying them. Those guards are stuck there unless they want to walk." Slocum went down and paid the same Apache he'd given the peso to.

The Apache put the money inside his shirt and held up the lead ropes. "Eat plenty good, huh?"

"*Sí.* Plenty good. Tomorrow, come back here early. I have more work."

They agreed, let out war whoops that made Slocum's blood turn cold, and galloped away.

"What were they all fired up about?" Dyke asked.

"I told them I had more work tomorrow," Slocum said.

"Steal more horses, huh?"

"Not a bad idea. On foot, Durango's bunch wouldn't be near as tough as they are on horseback."

"Who's on horseback?" Valdez asked, joining them.

"Not the damn guards at the pass. That's for sure, and the Apaches are having horse meat tonight," Dyke announced.

"Sounds good. What do we do next?" Valdez took a seat

at the table and ordered some breakfast from Benito, who had come out at his approach.

"Two of my army have slipped into the village down there," Slocum said after Benito had left. "I'm waiting to hear from them."

Valdez frowned. "Who are they?"

"Enrique Jimenez, the young man who came after us, and a woman who was our cook, Doña."

"I have heard Carlos Sanchez talk about Jimenez before, but this girl, who is she?"

"She used to live in the Madres and wanted to return here. She just offered to help him spy."

Valdez looked extremely upset by the information. "Dangerous business, you know, to spy on a man like Durango."

"I couldn't stop 'em." Slocum looked over his breakfast, which was delivered by a young barefoot boy. It smelled delicious. There were several folded flour tortillas on the side.

"I wish you'd've let me talk to them first," said Valdez.

Slocum glanced over at him. "They left our camp that morning before we met you."

Valdez shook his head. "We've lost so many good men down there—"

"They can take care of themselves," Slocum said, busy eating. "What is your stake in this?" he finally asked.

"My lovely wife is down there and I couldn't get her out."

Slocum nodded. That would upset anyone.

The guards looked nervous when Slocum studied them through his telescope's lens. They kept walking around, kicking at things, obviously upset. No doubt because Mateo had not returned from the night before, and also because of the loss of their horses a few hours earlier.

Had Enrique and Doña gone through there, or gone in by some back way? If he thought for one minute that they were in a life-or-death situation, he'd ride down there. And where was this man Sanchez? Enrique and Valdez had both spoken of him. But they'd never said where he was at. Slocum would ask Valdez later. For now, he wanted to watch these guards and wait for Enrique and Doña to return with some information about the valley. He needed to know Durango's strengths, and weaknesses if there were any.

Maybe he could get those guards drunk? Mateo had said they were a lazy lot. He needed a whiskey peddler to try to get by them. Where would he find one? Dyke—he'd do it. But the cantina had no whiskey. He folded up his brass scope, put it in the saddlebags, and then rode for town.

Buck and Dyke were on the patio. He saw them when he drew close. It was a cool day and clouds were gathering for an afternoon shower somewhere over the great range. He hurried up the stairs, and they poured him some wine when he reached the top. He dropped in a chair and considered the contents of the mug.

"Well?" Dyke asked. "What did you learn?"

"We need a barrel of whiskey. A small one to send up to those guards."

"Why waste good whiskey on that bunch?"

"Get them drunk and take them prisoner. We cut some more men out of Durango's bunch and we-have reduced his force greatly."

"Counting Mateo, that would make four." Buck bobbed his head as if considering it. "That ain't bad thinking. Let them get hollering drunk and then take 'em."

"But there ain't any whiskey," Dyke said in disgust. "Here anyhow."

"What's that barkeep's name?" Slocum asked, rising.

"Benito is what we call him," Buck said, sounding uncertain.

Slocum walked over to the cantina's side door. "Benito, are there any bootleggers around here?"

He gave Slocum an upset look. "Señor, they make such bad whiskey, I don't buy it."

It must be bad. "I'm not drinking this myself. I need a couple of jugs or a small barrel of it for bait."

"Bait?"

"I am not going fishing."

"I think I can send and get some."

With a pained look at the man, Slocum shook his head. "I need it *muy pronto*."

"*Sí, señor.* It will cost maybe four pesos."

"Here, buy it cheap as you can. I'll pay you and the messenger, too."

"Ah, *sí, señor.* If there is any, it will be here in a little while."

Slocum went back and dropped in his chair. "Firewater's coming."

"I'll be a son of a bitch. No whiskey for three days and you find it."

"This ain't whiskey he's buying, you old coot," Buck said with a scowl. "This is paint remover he's getting."

"Well, anyway." Dyke leaned back and studied the pine boughs overhead. "This sure ain't heaven, though it's high enough it makes my head swim at times."

"What else you figured out?" Buck shook his head at Dyke. "You got any smart ideas, Slocum?"

"If what Mateo told us was right, all we need to do is take the guards, and then stage a mock battle on the mountaintop so Durango sends some of his forces and we can bury them in their own trap."

"He can't afford to send many," Dyke said.

"Right. But if he loses another half dozen, he'll have no control."

"That's right." Buck lifted his mug. "Here's to finishing him off."

"Buck, it was a helluva lot easier last time we took him out," said Slocum.

"Naw. We were already in the valley and mad."

They all three laughed as Valdez returned. "Any word from your people?" he asked.

Slocum shook his head. "No. We have a new plan. We're going to have a fake battle in the pass. Get Durango to send his men and catch them in the trap they have set for us."

"How will we know if it will work?"

Slocum leaned back on the two back legs of the chair. "My Apaches are going to send us smoke signals from behind them."

"Huh?"

"We'll get the guards drunk and take them without firing a shot." Slocum dropped his chair down and scooted closer to the table. "Then we start shooting and letting off explosions that Durango will hear at the cantina, where I figure he is headquartered. He sends reinforcements. The Apaches will signal us when they are coming and bam, we blow the damn mountain up on them."

"What if he runs instead?"

"Good riddance. Do you have a better plan?"

Valdez shook his head.

Slocum could see the man was not convinced about the plan. Even with his wife down there in harm's way, he acted uncertain about everything they wanted to do. Like he didn't want to shake the apple tree because someone might get hurt. Hell with him.

Something must have gone wrong for Doña and Enrique. The thought of what might have happened made his stomach roil.

17

The woman came to see him late that afternoon. From his grape arbor shade he saw her coming, and sat up to view her crossing the stream. She removed her sandals with her back erect—no sitting on her ass on the ground, knees up and spread apart, to take them off. She carried them in one hand and the skirt hem in the other, and like a fine horse made dainty steps in the swift water. Never losing her balance or staggering around like those clumsy washerwomen who often fell in. She had what he called real class.

"Captain," Tomas called to him.

"I see her."

"*Sí.* I am sending the change of the guards to the east pass in the morning."

"Fine." He didn't give a fuck about that business—Señora Valdez was coming.

"Good afternoon," she said, taking the chair he held out for her at his table.

He went around and sat down with a nod. José brought a fine glass and uncorked a bottle of wine for her.

"Thank you," she said to him as he poured some wine in the fine-stemmed glass.

"Always my pleasure, Señora." He bowed and left them.

She laughed, holding the stem in her fingers. "I bet he does not have many of these."

Durango threw his head back and laughed. "They would be hard to get here in one piece, no?"

"Very hard. Many things are shattered coming here." Then, with a toss of her fine hair, she looked seriously at him. "I hope there are no more incidents like that rape."

He rose and leaned his arm up on a post to look across the stream. "Yes. I don't understand men who do that to little girls. They must be mad. I planned to kick and beat him till he would never consider it again."

"I know. I know it happens—but . . ."

He turned back to look at her.

She was dabbing tears on her cheeks. Then, with a slight sniff, she sat up even straighter. "I have thirty-two students thanks to Tomas's urging."

"He's a good man, isn't he?"

"An excellent truant officer."

He turned his palms up at her. "What is that? *Tyrant* officer?"

"In many countries they have a policeman that catches children skipping school and drags them to class with a kick in the seat of their pants for good measure."

"Ah, Tomas, you have a new job now," he shouted.

His man stuck his head out the door. "What is that, Captain?"

"Tyrant officer?"

"No," she said softly. "True—ant."

"Whatever. You are supposed to get the little children that skip school and make them go to classes."

"*Sí,* Captain, I will watch for them."

"See there," he said to her. "You have one now. He will do it." What else could he do to please her? He was getting worked up just talking to her. Damn, she could have anything she wanted for one thing—to sleep in his bed.

Maybe he would even go to her casa in secret if she feared

rumors or losing favor with the padre when he came. All he wanted was to make love to her. It was all he could think about. He always took what he wanted—but he wanted her willing—willing to be his lover, not his slave.

"Is there any way to get some slate boards and chalk for my students to write on?" she asked.

"I don't know. I will see, Señora."

"Thank you. I know you are busy, Señor. I am grateful for the children and the school. I must get home now and make my lessons for tomorrow."

"Come again, Señora. I like to talk to you. You are the sunshine in my day."

"Thank you." She excused herself and left him leaning his forearm on a post and his feverish forehead against it. Damn, he wanted that woman.

Where was her husband? How could he be gone so long away from her? Maybe he did not appreciate what he possessed in her.

That evening before dark, he rode over to stop at the mayor's casa. Lupe came to the doorway in a dress that exposed her long breasts. She stood just inside and used her hand to protect her eyes from the setting sun's glare behind him.

"So finally you come to see how I am?" she said with a curl of her lip.

He dismounted and wrapped the reins around the polished hitch rack. There were times he wanted to smack her smart mouth. This was such a time, but he was in no mood for the ensuing argument that would bring on.

Trying to act weary, he shook his head. "I have been busy. It is not easy to run this place."

She retreated inside.

"What have you to eat?" He looked around, following her in.

"To eat?" She frowned at him suspiciously as she backed up to the table.

"Food. Some wine. What do you have?" Crowding close to her, he lowered his hand and felt her pubic mound under the skirt. He whispered in her ear, "I want some play, then we can eat."

"*Sí. Sí.* Whatever you say—"

His mouth closed on hers, cut off her words, and he crushed her to his chest. She would be sore again when he left her. Like a pump that needed little priming, she clung tight to him as they kissed, and he soon became heady with a need for her. He pushed her to her knees before him and fumbled with the buttons to open his pants. Then his half-erect aching pecker sprang out. She took it and began to lick the head and stroke it. His hand kept her head in place as she began to orally accept it.

The world swirled around him. His hips ached to drive his shaft down her throat. Then her tongue began to rasp his erection on the underside. He pumped it faster and faster until it exploded and the white cum ran from both corners of her mouth. A smile crept over his mouth—she looked good like that. The horny bitch.

She wiped most of it off on the back of her hand and rose slowly. "I am pleased you came, Durango. I missed you so. I knew you must have needed me—" She hugged him around the waist. "I have some beans and can make some tortillas."

"Do that." He began buttoning his pants and shaking his leg to get his deflated dick back in place.

Soon, she was busy making a tortilla, patting it out between her palms in a circular fashion. "You have missed me, I can tell."

He nodded, not interested in her chatter. An evening with her might solve his horniness. Maybe after this, he could make love to the señora instead of this skinny nymphomaniac. Damn, he wondered if Slocum was ever coming. He wanted that over, too. Slocum in a shallow grave would be such a triumph.

He rubbed his hand on his upper leg. Was he hungry for food or another toss in the hammock with her? Better eat first. He'd be all night satisfying her. He closed his eyes and he could see a picture of Señora Valdez crossing the stream. Such a woman.

Before dawn, he left Lupe asleep in her hammock. Groggy and stiff, he dressed in the darkness, put on on his gun and sombrero, then went for his horse. He rode up to the cantina in the dim purple light and Tomas ran out.

His man said, "A boy brought us a note from Palo Alto."

"What does it say?"

"Two spies. Watch the pass."

"What does it mean?"

Tomas shook his head. "I was on my way to look for you."

"Where is this boy that brought it?"

"He rode away after he asked if I'd give this to you."

"You know this boy?"

"No. I have never seen him before."

"Damnit, is this a trap or for real?"

"I don't know, Captain. He said it was only for you. He had came a long ways, his horse was heaving he was so hot."

"Did you send those fresh guards to the pass?"

"*Sí*, they left a short while ago. That will make seven men up there."

"Mateo knows how to explode the mountain?"

"*Sí*, Captain. He is a good man. He won't wilt under a little fire. Tough hombre."

"Why does he stay up there all the time?"

"He was angry about some of our men raping small girls when we first came here."

"What was that to him? Oh, forget it. Let us find some breakfast. I am starved."

"*Sí*, Captain."

While they ate Nalda's eggs, salsa, goat cheese, and tortillas, Durango pointed his wrap at Tomas. "I want you to

look for any strangers in the valley. Two spies means there
are two here. Find them."

"I will. I will if they are here."

"I am going to nap a while. Wake me up when you find
them or learn something."

"If there are spies in this valley, I will find them."

"Eat your food. They can wait that long."

"*Sí*, Captain."

Durango had no idea how long he had slept, but a loud
explosion woke him. He threw his feet over the edge of the
bed and blinked at the ashen-faced José in the doorway.

"There has been—much shooting going on up at the
pass. I wanted to wake you. But I didn't know—"

"Where is Tomas?"

"I have not seen him, Señor. Since you ate with him earlier."

Bare-assed, Durango rushed outside and looked up at the
distant pass. Two columns of smoke rose to the sky. Was
Slocum at the pass? He hurried back inside.

"José, sound the trumpet. I need all the men."

"I am not as good—"

"Fuck that. Blow it with all your might." He hustled the
man outside.

Another loud explosion rolled across the valley. Son of
a bitch. Did they have a cannon, too?

18

Slocum licked his chapped lips in the predawn. They'd been over the entire mountain and examined all the charges. Dyke, who knew something about blowing up mountains, thought the charges would launch a huge landslide. But they'd save that to bury Durango.

Dawn struck, and Slocum saw three puffs of smoke from a place about where he thought his Apaches would be. It was repeated.

"See that?" Buck asked, out of breath from climbing uphill, and pointed westward.

"No doubt that's the replacements coming."

"I thought so."

"There is a rider coming," Dyke shouted.

"Stop him," Slocum said. "We need all the information anyone has got."

Buck and Dyke halted the boy on the lathered horse coming out of the valley. The animal's breath rasped in and out. Buck jerked the youth of twelve or so off the horse and set him on his feet.

"Who are you?"

"Carlo."

"Where in the hell you been in such a rush?"

The boy didn't answer. Buck jerked him up. "Tell me. Where have you been?"

"Antonio."

"What for?"

The boy hesitated and then dropped his chin. "To take a message to Durango."

"What did it say?"

"I don't know—I can't read."

"What did he say?"

The boy shook his head about to cry. "Nothing. He was asleep."

"You delivered it?"

"To a man—" The boy swallowed. "Who said he was his—assistant."

"Tomas," Buck mumbled.

Slocum agreed. "Whose fine horse is this you have wind-broke?" He walked around the boy.

"If I tell you, he will kill my mother."

Buck blinked at Slocum. "Who's he talking about?"

"Me," Valdez said, walking up. "I sent Durango a note so that I could ransom my wife."

"Why now?" Slocum asked.

"I was hoping she might escape and if not, then I wanted her out of harm's way. Your plans to take the valley will put her in the line of fire."

"What did you say to him?" Slocum asked.

"I offered Durango a large sum for her safe delivery."

Slocum was in deep doubt. "I wished you'd talked with us first."

"Your wife is not down there. I have gone crazy for months. If something happens to her, I won't ever forgive myself. I had to risk something."

Slocum turned to the others. "Set the fires and let off that big explosion. I want him to think his men are fighting a helluva battle up here. Maybe he'll send more men."

"Can I talk you out of this?" Valdez asked.

Slocum whirled around and looked him in the eye. "No. I'll thank you to send no more communications to him. I am also asking you to leave this area since I do not trust you, sir."

"Trust me? Why, I've lost a fortune fighting this bastard. And my wife—"

"I know she is down there. But so are my friends and many others who have lost husbands and their loved ones. You better leave now and we can discuss this when the whole thing is over."

"All I wanted—"

"Damnit to hell, get out of my sight," Slocum said.

The explosion rocked the mountain and dust was everywhere. Valdez led off his tired horse. Good riddance.

Carlo followed him, leading his own horse.

Dyke was shouting. "Your Apaches must be driving the replacements at us. Hear them kii-yipping?"

"Good, we can count them as out of the game."

Dyke caught his arm. "You think Valdez warned Durango?"

Slocum shook his head. "Hard to tell who your real enemies are at times, Dyke. I don't know, but I don't like it one bit."

"They're riding up here like their pants are on fire," Buck said.

"Good, welcome them."

"Get your hands up," Buck ordered as the three wide-eyed outlaws reined in their horses at the pole gate.

"Fucking Apaches are after us." One pointed back behind them.

Slocum walked over and nodded at them. "I pay them five bucks apiece for your kind, dead or alive."

"Who in the hell are you, hombre?"

"My name's Slocum. Now get over here. Keep those hands behind your head. Dyke, search them for weapons."

"Wait till Durango hears about this. You've only got three guys up here and you got the guards and us prisoners? Man, that will burn his ass and he'll be up here to whip the shit out of you three."

"Listen." Slocum went over and grabbed his shirt and jerked him up. "Buck and I alone put that sumbitch in jail and the rest of his gang in the grave or jail here the last time by ourselves."

"Yeah, well, you'll see when he brings his men up here."

"How many men? Five or six?"

"I'm telling you, don't mess with Durango."

Slocum shoved him back in line. "I've got to go pay my Apaches."

"Well, that's fifteen dollars I owe you," he said as the Apaches rode up, and held out his hand with the money.

The older one took it. "More come to boom party?" he asked. Slocum and his friends called him Padre and the younger Red Boy since their Apache names were too hard to say.

"They may. Run them this way," Slocum said.

"Apaches can do that." He raised his older-model Winchester skyward with his right hand and went to coyote-yipping. The two rode off down the mountain.

"Hell," Dyke said. "Them red devils are having themselves a ball."

Slocum agreed.

When all the prisoners were tied up, Slocum asked them where Durango was at. They all sulked and no one answered.

"I want some answers. You better speak up or I'll let them Apaches roast your balls."

When they did not immediately answer him, he went over and kicked the nearest outlaw in the leg.

"Hell, he was asleep when we left this morning," the short one said.

"Someone delivered him a note this morning. Any of you hear about it?"

Heads shook.

"You know a Mrs. Valdez?"

"Yeah, we worked three days fixing a fucking school for her."

"A what?"

"She's his pet. Rich bitch, she must screw real good. He quit the mayor's wife over her."

Heads nodded in agreement. Were she and Durango having an affair? Did Valdez know about the school? No telling. Slocum needed to go down there and find Enrique and Doña. He was tired of the mountaintop and worried about his people.

"What do you think?" Buck asked Slocum when they walked away from the prisoners to talk it over.

"He don't send any more reinforcements up here soon, I'm going in there tonight and see what I can learn."

"Count me in."

"You better stay here and help Dyke. I'm not satisfied with this Valdez business. Something's fishy there."

"We're in a trap. Six prisoners now and no one but us to guard 'em." Buck shook his head in disgust.

"I'll ride in and come back out. If those Apaches weren't afraid of the dark, I'd take them along."

"Would they stay and guard the prisoners?" Buck pointed to a large golden eagle soaring out over the canyon.

"That's an idea." Slocum watched the eagle coast on the updrafts. "I wish we had wings so we could fly down there."

"You're worried about Enrique and Doña?"

"Yes, and not knowing a damn thing don't make it easier."

"You going to ride down and ask them Apaches?"

"Naw, they'll be up here before sundown. Then we can decide what we're doing."

"You thinking like I am, Slocum? That by this time, if he ain't answered all those blasts and his men going off that shift not returning, he's not going to come up here?"

"Hard to imagine what he thinks. Durango is sly in many cruel ways, and whatever he's doing, I sure don't know. He may have packed up already and taken a powder, or maybe he has more traps set up for us to stumble into like the landslide he planned for here."

"What are we doing now?" Dyke asked in a low voice, glancing back at the prisoners.

"Slocum wants to go down there tonight and learn what he can about our two friends," Buck said.

"What do we do with the prisoners?"

"Get the Apaches to watch them until we get back," Slocum said.

"Why, the prisoners'll shit all over themselves if we leave them with the Apaches."

"Aw, hell, let 'em do it."

"Jokes aside. There's something wrong, or Enrique or Doña or both would have been back here by now," Slocum said.

"You're probably right," Dyke said. "That boy busted his ass to get you two to save those people down there. Doña's straight as an arrow."

"I may start down there now," Slocum said. "I'll send the Apaches back and then you two can follow. I'll meet you around midnight north of the cantina at that spring that flows into the stream."

"Be careful," Buck said.

"Yeah, we'd both hate digging a damn grave," Dyke said, and laughed.

Slocum started for the dun horse and stopped. "Tell those Apaches not to trust Valdez. I'm not certain of his part in all this, but he worries me."

Buck agreed, and so did Dyke.

Slocum rode off down into the canyon, the whole time imagining the avalanche of rocks and boulders that would cascade down on anyone on the trail when the charges were set off. The trail soon joined the stream that was fed by other streams as well as by springs to form the lifeline for the small community below.

The Apaches rode out of a side canyon and met him on the trail. He quickly explained his plan, and they agreed to guard the prisoners. Satisfied the matter was handled, he rode on as the sun sank casting long shadows over the land. The two bucks raced off to replace his men as guards. Riding along, he about chuckled over Dyke's concern that those outlaws might be that scared. Serve them right after all the murdering that had gone on.

He took a less-used path away from the stream in case there was a guard on the road. The way proved rougher, but also offered more cover in the brush and trees. Twilight was fading when he crossed the spring branch he planned to meet Buck and Dyke at. Soon he was riding in starlight and trying to remember the canyon where the old funeral vault was located.

After two false starts up wrong canyons, he found the right one, hitched the gun on his hip, and set the dun horse up the path. Letting the dun pick his way through the tall pines, he passed through some places that were dark as a mine. Then he rode into the open again in pearl light that bathed the towering walls.

He spotted the yawning mouth of the vault. It appeared to be open. Damn. Off his horse, he dropped the reins. The dun was ground-reined and would remain there. Slocum hurried up the slope and found the door of the vault wide open. Too late.

Lighting a match, he looked over the interior. A disassembled Gatling gun was piled on the floor, along with several rounds of ammo for it. Then he struck another match. The well-made wooden box had stamped on the side the Spanish words for Federal Mint of Mexico. That must have been Durango's source of funds.

Durango had fled the coop. Damn, Slocum should have come sooner. Everyone should be grateful—the butcher of Antonio was gone.

Where were Enrique and Doña? If Durango had killed them, Slocum would search the entire earth for his rotten soul. Meanwhile, he'd better go back and meet the others.

19

How long would it take Slocum to bring his army over the pass if his plan to blow up the mountain failed? Durango scratched his ear. Something was wrong—no one had come back. His army was assembling outside—five sleepy men. Those five and the three on the south gate were all he had left. Where was Tomas?

Looking for spies. Durango stomped outside and asked if any of them had seen his man in the past hour. They shrugged.

"Get on your horses, spread out, and find him. We have much to do and little time. Also, when you come back, bring every stout pack animal there is and bring all the packsaddles, too. We have much to haul."

They began to move, and he went to find the stable boy. He told him to put packsaddles on all the horses left. Then he went back to the cantina, leading his gray stallion Eagle, and hitched him to the rack.

"Bring me mescal, José, and some lunch," he said, seated at a table. He was uncertain if he could eat, but he knew it might be his last chance to do so for some time.

"Mescal and a glass, *patrón*," José said, setting both on the table. "Nalda is taking a siesta, but I will wake her."

"Do that. Where did Tomas go?" He drummed his fingernails on the tabletop.

"I am not sure."

Durango nodded. He watched the man rush off to wake the *puta* that worked for him. Where was Tomas?

He heard a horse clambering across the rocks and the stream. He rushed to the doorway. Miguel leaped off his horse and ran up the steps. "Durango, Durango. Tomas is dead!"

"What? Who did it?"

"We don't know. We are asking everyone."

"Madre de Dios, who would have killed Tomas?" He mounted his horse, sick to his stomach, and set out with Miguel, who was pounding his heels on his slower horse to keep up.

There were shots ahead, and Durango cross-whipped Eagle with the reins. He could see one of his men lying facedown on the ground. It wasn't Tomas. Another sat in the road holding his bloody arm. Durango drew his pistol and rushed forward. A man charged out of the doorway to shoot at him, but his pistol clicked on empty.

Durango fired over Eagle's head, and his second shot spun the man around as he was reloading in the doorway. Durango reined Eagle up and shot the man again. This time his bullet struck him in the face; he jerked back and collapsed. Then, out of the house, came a short woman with a small pistol shooting at him. Her first shot smacked into Eagle's neck. The stallion reared, and two more shots from her pistol slapped into his horse. Eagle fell sideways and crashed down, pinning Durango's leg under him with a shock of pain that jolted him so hard he was unable to move.

Then he saw her angry face as she advanced on him, aiming the pistol. With the hammer cocked and pointed at him, she spit out, "Die, you killer of children."

Then rifles and pistols from all around cut her down, and

despite the sharp pain in his leg, Durango breathed again. That was too close.

"Who was she?" he demanded as his men rushed over to get the horse off him.

"We don't know her. The one you shot in the doorway was Enrique Jimenez. He was from the village," Martinez said. "One of the rebels."

"Go easy, you are killing my leg," he shouted as they tried to pull the dead stallion off him with reatas tied to then saddle horns of two of their horses.

Durango broke into a sweat. Pain made his sight fuzzy. "Where did that bitch come from?"

"I guess with Jimenez."

"Ah," Durango moaned in pain as Miguel moved around him trying to lift or roll the horse off his leg. The other two men were on horseback trying to find a way to help.

"We will need the guards from the south end," Durango said. "Send a boy after them. How is the wounded one over there?"

"His arm is shattered. He'll lose it."

"Damn, how long have those two been here?"

Miguel shrugged. "Only God would know, Señor."

"You are certain that Tomas is dead?"

"He is lying on the ground up the road. Yes, he is dead. We found those two had hid in that jacal." Miguel strained to help lift Eagle's weight from him, and the ropes grew taunt as the horses dug in.

Durango let out a cry. Their efforts were killing him. Then, at last, the weight of the horse was off him and he bent over in sharp pain to hug his leg. It was broken.

He sat on his butt. Slocum and his army were coming. He must leave. Tomas was dead.

"Get some sticks and bind my leg." Jolts of pain ran over his face. He dropped back on his hands. "Miguel." He motioned him close.

"We must load all we can from that crypt in the canyon.

Here is the key. You know what to load. If we must leave things, leave the Gatling gun and any explosives."

"I can handle that. Do not worry, we will care for you."

Durango pulled him down by the sleeve. "This was the work of that bastard Slocum. Someone warned me these fucking spies were here—I never thought they would kill Tomas—hurry, that bastard is coming . . ."

Miguel nodded and ran for his horse. He rode out of there whipping the horse in a trail of dust. With no way to stand, Durango sat on his butt and fretted. Could Miguel load all the treasure and get back to him in time? Who was this bitch who about shot him? He'd never seen her before that he could recall.

An older woman brought him a weaved rug that she spread out for him on the ground. He thanked her, and moved over to it on his butt and hands as he dragged his leg.

"I need my leg splinted."

She nodded. But he wasn't certain from her blank face if she knew what he meant. Without a word, she nodded again and went off. He eased himself down on his back, but that was no way to escape the throbbing in his leg.

In a short while, three women came with a bundle of sticks and some rope. A hawk-faced woman looked at his foot like a butcher did a chunk of meat to see how to chop it up. He sat up and put his arms behind him to brace himself.

"I will try to set it," she said, on her knees at the end of the rug. "I must pull off the boot. Your foot is already swelling."

"Yes."

Lifting it into her lap, she began to try to get the boot off. Beads of sweat popped out on his face. Her efforts hurt worse than removing the horse. She stopped.

"Maybe I should cut it off?"

Through his fuzzy vision, he nodded at her to go ahead and do that. To be so helpless, seated on his butt in the middle of the road in horrific pain. They could take the treasure and ride out without him. And Slocum could find him sitting there with three old women doctoring him. Maybe he should do like that *puta* Marisel did—put the gun in his mouth and blow his brains out. Time was short.

She split the boot down the side with a sharp knife, and he could feel relief in his lower leg and foot as she worked down. When the boot was cut open and his swollen calf popped out, the other two women sucked in their breath in shock.

Then she eased the boot off and set it aside. Her coal black eyes looked hard at him. "Now I must set the bones."

He closed his eyes. "I know. Do you have anything? Mescal? Laudanum?" He looked from her to the other two. The first old woman, who'd brought him the rug, squatted down beside him. She smelled of wood smoke and a strong woman's musk. From her apron pocket, she took out something and held it between her forefinger and thumb.

"What the hell is it?"

"Peyote."

For a minute, he hesitated. Then he nodded, and she put it in his mouth. It tasted like dirt. Gritty-tasting like ground sand on his molars as he chewed it. Pinpoints of bright light began to dazzle his vision like fireworks. Powerful stuff—he looked down at her—she was a mile away from him. He hoped she could hear him. "Set the leg . . ."

20

Slocum waited in the dark, hearing horses coming from the direction of the pass. At last. That must be them. Sitting on the dun, he whistled.

"Slocum?" Buck called out.

"Yes. Come on." He pushed his horse out into the clearing. "He may have flown the coop. That burial vault is empty save for a Gatling gun, ammo, and some blasting explosives."

"He left, huh?" Dyke said, looking around in the night. "No sign of Enrique and Doña?"

Slocum shook his head. "I'm not sure what's happened, but we can wake up the man who owns the cantina and see what he knows."

"Cantina operators know everything," Dyke agreed.

"Let's go find him," Slocum said. His heart was heavy. If Durango was gone, where were Enrique and Doña?

"His name's José," Buck said. "Unless there's a new one."

"That was it," Slocum agreed.

They dismounted at a distance and hitched their horses. Checking their revolvers, they headed for the dark cantina. Slocum slipped into the dark side room where the man slept and moved to the bed. The small figure under the blanket was not a man.

Slocum looked around in the darkness. There was no one else in there. He clamped a hand over the woman's mouth and whispered in her ear, "Be very quiet."

Her eyes flew open, and even in the dim light he could see she was shocked. "Where is José?"

"Outside in a hammock. Who are you?"

"Slocum."

"We heard you were coming. Durango is gone." When he released her, she sat up naked to the waist. In the dim light, her flabby breasts looked flattened.

"There were two friends of mine," Slocum said. "Enrique Jimenez and a girl named Doña."

She crossed herself and scooted toward him. "I am sorry, Señor, but they may be dead."

"Dead?"

"Sí. They say Enrique shot Tomas, Durango's man, and then died trying to kill Durango."

"Doña?"

"She tried to kill him, too, they say. All the bodies are at the church."

"Bodies?"

"Sí, they killed another of Durango's men besides Tomas in the shoot-out." As if she'd decided he had no interest in her body, she began to pull on her skirt.

"What's happened?" Buck asked from the open door.

"The lady—"

"My name is Nalda. I work here."

"Buck's mine. That's Dyke."

"Nalda says she thinks both of them were killed in a gunfight here."

"Aw, hell," Dyke swore.

"I knew something was wrong yesterday," she said, fighting a knit sweater over her head and then covering herself. She lit a candle, which dimly illuminated the room. "A boy brought Durango a message in the morning about those two spies being here."

Slocum exchanged a look with Buck and Dyke, then turned back to her. "Was he a boy of twelve or so?"

She laughed and nodded. "He was so scared, he rode off before Durango's man could talk to him."

"You read the note?"

She shook her head. "I can't read. Neither could Durango. Tomas told him. Two spies. Trouble in the pass."

"Not a word about ransoming a woman?"

"No. Here is José."

The sleepy-eyed man shuffled into the room, scratching his belly through his shirt. "What can I do for you?"

"Did you read the note that Durango received yesterday from the boy?"

"Tomas got it and let Durango sleep a little. I never read it, but like Nalda, I heard what he told Durango. Two spies and trouble at the pass." The bartender stretched and spoke to her. "Make us some coffee and food. These two men are the ones that put Durango in jail the last time."

"Why would that no-account traitor send Durango a note?" Dyke asked.

"Too many things unanswered," Slocum said.

"You know," Nalda said, "that woman who came here with Jimenez shot Durango's horse and it fell on him. They say he broke his leg very bad. A woman set it and they took him out of here on a stretcher between two horses."

José nodded. "He was high on peyote and drinking mescal for the pain, too."

"I'd've peyoted that son of a bitch," Dyke said.

"Are the bodies in the church?" Slocum asked.

"*Sí, señor,*" she said. "The door is unlocked. I can get you a lamp."

"Nalda, you fix the food and coffee. I can show him," José said.

"*Sí,* I just wanted to help."

Slocum and his men all thanked her as they followed José out.

"I will have lots of food ready when you get back," she promised them from the doorway.

"*Gracias,*" Slocum said, and turned to José. "Is there a Señora Valdez here?"

"*Sí,* she is the wonderful woman that opened the school."

"Where does she live?"

"Up the road across the stream."

"Durango ever talk of holding her hostage?"

"Hostage?" José laughed aloud. "She came often to see him, and made him open the school. She is a beautiful woman. But she is not a woman to touch. You know what I mean?"

"Durango never touched her?"

At the tall, ornate door to the small chapel, the man stopped and smiled. "He wanted to, but he wanted her to come to him."

"I'll have to meet this lady."

They removed their hats and entered the dark interior. The candle lamp illuminated the stations of the cross on each wall. Small candles on racks burned in the front. Four coffins were lined up in the front of the church.

Slocum lifted the cloth off the first one. He did not know the man.

"Ortega. He was a bandit," the cantina man said.

Slocum moved to the second coffin and raised the shroud. It contained Tomas's remains, no mistaking his sharp features. The next one he exposed was Enrique, and the dark bullet hole in his forehead made him look stark.

Slocum wet his lips and moved away from the coffins.

"You don't want to see Doña?" Dyke asked.

"No. I want to remember her as the sweet girl that joined us to get a chance to go home." Slocum beat his hat against his leg.

Dyke nodded. "Good idea."

Buck peeked at her, and then he turned away looking sick. "It's her all right. What now?"

"Durango's getting away."

Dyke and Buck nodded.

"We riding after 'em?" he asked the pair.

"We don't go after them, they'll be back here and be worse the next time," Buck said. "You wasn't figuring on going after them?"

"Oh, I was going. I just wondered if you two wanted to."

"I want that sumbitch dead," Dyke said. Then realizing he was in a church, he shook his head in disapproval and started for the door.

"So does God," Slocum said, stepping outside. "They can't go fast with all those pack animals. We'll catch them."

"What about the prisoners?" Buck asked. "Them Apaches may eat them if we don't go up there and do something." Dyke said, "I ain't losing any sleep over them. But we left that kind of in the Apaches' hands."

"Buck, what do we need to do with them?" Slocum asked.

"Damned if I know. The damn *federales* are so corrupt these days, I doubt they'd do anything to 'em."

"Turn them loose?"

"Hell, they'd just take over some other valley or go back to robbing and killing."

"Should they be shot?"

"I reckon."

"Then we've got to do that first and then find Durango."

"Hell, we're burning daylight," Dyke said.

They mounted up, and José stopped them. "Have some food first. Nalda will have it ready. Then go do what you must do."

They agreed and stopped at the cantina. It was just before dawn when they finished eating and paid her. Then they rode out.

Slocum was weary, bone-tired, but he knew there was nothing he could do but ride on and deal with the prisoners.

They reached the pass by noontime. The older Apache, Padre, came to meet them.

"Everything all right?" Slocum asked.

"Fine. You need us anymore?"

"Where are the prisoners?" Slocum looked around.

"Your man came and got them."

"My man? Oh, Valdez. What did he do with them?"

The Apache made a pistol with his hand and said "bang" a couple of times.

Dyke shook his head and looked at the sky for help. Buck gripped his saddle horn and did the same.

"Then what?" Slocum asked the Apache.

"He had two men with a wagon haul them away."

Slocum nodded, and wondered what he needed to do about Valdez. "We're going to track down the outlaw chief. You two want to go along and scout?"

The Apaches agreed with big grins.

"Buck, take them and get a couple of mules from the mine to pack the food. That's all we'll need. Dyke and I are going to find Valdez. He has some explaining to do. Meet you at the cantina."

Buck agreed, and told the Apaches something in their language and they laughed.

Slocum and Dyke set out to find Valdez.

"Slocum, we don't even know where he lives," said Dyke.

"How many places can he live in this small village?"

"We can ask Benito at the cantina."

They found the bartender a few minutes later busy washing mugs.

"Where does Valdez live?" Dyke asked him.

"Oh, the señor has gone to Mexico City."

"Huh? When did he leave for there?" Slocum asked.

"A couple of hours ago. He said he had to see some mining company about their needs for a new mine."

"You knew he executed those six bandits?" Slocum asked.

"Yes. He said that Sanchez told him to do that."

"Was this man Sanchez here?"

Benito shook his head. "If he was, I never saw him."

"Why did he kill them?"

Benito stopped washing dishes. "I don't know and I don't ask."

"Tell me about his wife."

"They don't live together."

"They're separated?" Dyke asked.

"I guess."

"But he told me he was concerned that Durango might hold her for ransom."

Benito laughed. "Maybe Valdez would pay him to keep her."

"That bad, huh?" Dyke asked.

Benito smiled.

"Come on, we have a bandit to catch," Slocum said to Dyke. "Thanks, Benito."

Outside, going down the stone steps to their horses, Dyke glanced back. "Strange deal. Shoots six worthless bandits in cold blood and then he goes to Mexico City. Don't make sense."

Slocum agreed. "We may never know about the man."

They mounted up to go meet Buck and the Apaches and then ride after Durango.

It was past midnight when they rode up to Antonio. The Chinese candles were lit and the music wafted out from the cantina. It looked very peaceful, and they decided to stop and see if there was any word about their man.

A cheer from the people assembled went up when they came in the door. "Did you find him?" José shouted.

Slocum shook his head. "We'll get them."

"Nalda, get them some food. They must be hungry," José said to her.

Slocum was about to sit down when a man came inside and went over to him. "There is someone outside who wants to talk to you."

Slocum frowned at him.

"She won't hurt you."

He gave a sign to the others that it was all right, and went out the door. Under the starlight he looked around. Who was she and what did she want?

"I am over here, Señor."

She was seated at a table under the arbor. He removed his hat and she indicated a chair opposite hers.

"Good evening. My name is Slocum, but I don't know yours."

"My name is Juanita Valdez."

"What can I do for you, Señora?"

"Let's not be formal. Juanita is fine. I am very sorry about your losses. For too short a time, I knew both of them—Enrique and Doña Maria Salaras."

"I never knew her last name."

"She told me how brave you were. How you didn't have a thing to gain by coming up here except your honor."

He could barely see much of her besides her straight back in the filtered starlight. "She was easily impressed."

"No. She, too, was brave."

"You know, Juanita, there are things in this world that need doing. If they ain't anyone else's job, then it's yours."

"My, you are profound. I am amazed. Tell me, what will you do now?"

"Go find Durango and either bury him or deliver him to the officials."

"You've done that before and it didn't work. They turned him loose."

He shrugged, listening to the soft music coming from the cantina. "Do you dance?"

"I guess I can."

"Good. I'd rather dance than talk." He took her in his arms and they slowly began to dance. She was tall, with a willowy figure, and easy to dance with.

"Is your husband mad?" he asked, not looking down at her.

"There are times I suspect he is. I understand you met him."

"I never knew if he was on this side or my side."

"He has some serious mental problems, so we don't live together."

"Couldn't you get it annulled in the Church?"

She shrugged and threw her head back. "I bear my own burdens."

"He's very smart, I understand."

She readjusted her hand on his shoulder. "I would rather dance, too."

He gave her a hug and a smile. "I won't probe.

"I want to say your kindness to Doña will not go unrewarded."

He spun her around and brought her back against him when the music stopped. And he kissed her. It soon became more than that, and they both were flush-faced when they split apart. He pulled her tight against his body.

"Let me come back," he said, smelling her lilac perfume. "When this is over. When we have some time to savor each other."

She exhaled slowly. "I haven't been that stirred up in years—yes, I would enjoy that even more. I shall wait for your return."

Later, he slept a few hours by himself rolled up in two blankets against the mountain night's chill. At dawn, he roused his partners, Buck, Dyke, and the two Apaches, and they ate the breakfast Nalda had promised them.

With the horses saddled and the mules packed, they rode south, Slocum confident they could not lose the bandits with the two Apaches reading sign. They trotted hard all day. Obviously, the trail led out of the Madres and off the western slope.

They found two of the bandits' previous camps, and the horse apples on the trail were looking fresher.

"There's a village called Santo Cristoforo west of here in the foothills," Slocum said.

"They would be there tonight at the speed they travel," the old Apache, Padre, said. His partner agreed.

"Then we will push on and catch them there."

The day passed swiftly. The trail grew steep and the crunch of gravel under hooves filled Slocum's ears. A shrill cry of a hawk soaring overhead filled the deep canyon as they descended down the side of the deep gorge on a narrow one-horse-wide shelf.

Slocum tried to ignore the right side. From time to time, his stirrup scuffed the wall side. The torturous way down kept him anxious to be on solid ground. How did they ever get Durango off this mountain on a sling between two animals? To judge from the tracks, that was how Durango's men must have carried him out of the valley.

The sun had dropped to the western horizon when Slocum at last reined up, swept his right leg over the dun's rump, and stood on solid ground. Even the unemotional Apaches looked pleased. The last ray of golden sunlight shone on the completed tower of the church further down the valley and the small village that surrounded it.

"You been to Santo Cristoforo before?" he asked the old man.

Padre nodded.

"You and Buck go see what you can learn about them. There's water here for the stock, and we'll make camp."

The Apache agreed. He and Buck remounted and rode on with Slocum's warning to be careful.

Slocum and Dyke began to unpack the mules, and the younger Indian, Red Boy, fell in and helped.

"Reckon they're here?" Dyke asked.

"I think so," Slocum said, wondering how many of them

were left. One of them had been wounded, and Durango's leg had been badly shattered by the horse falling on him.

Time would tell.

"Is that the only way back out of here?" Slocum asked Red Boy.

"No, good way over there." He waved to the south.

Dyke looked at the sky. "Oh, hell, that damn mountain must have taken ten years off my life."

They all three laughed.

Slocum looked back toward the village bathed in twilight. He hoped they were there.

21

Dyke had cooked a sliced slab of bacon for something quick. Seated on the ground at the fire, Slocum heard horses coming. He set his tin plate aside and rose. On his feet, he shifted the six-gun in place.

"It is them," Red Boy said.

Slocum marveled. How that young buck knew, he wasn't sure, because Red Boy never stood up to look. In fact, he never stopped eating his frijoles. Must be some sense that they naturally possessed.

"They're here in a camp at the edge of the village," Buck said, dropping down heavily with a ring of his spur rowels.

"How many?"

"Five or six healthy ones. Durango was asleep on a pallet. There's another man there that's in bad shape. Some doctor had been there and was leaving when we first peeked at them."

"What do you think?"

"I think about dawn we can take them easy."

"Good. Draw us a map on the ground."

Squatted on his heels, Buck showed them all the ground features in the firelight.

When they finished, Dyke brought them plates of crisp bacon.

"Is there any law here?" Slocum asked,

Padre shrugged.

"What do you mean by law?" Buck asked.

"If we make this raid, I want that stolen money they have for the people of Antonio. Crooked authorities would only confiscate it for themselves."

Everyone agreed.

"So we need to take care of Durango, locate the money, and pack it and get the hell out of there. That means have these mules loaded and ready to take along, too."

"That's a damn good idea," Dyke said, sipping his coffee.

"Padre, how do we get out of here and not take that damn canyon?"

Buck stopped eating and blinked in disbelief.

"Mine road is that way." The Apache waved to the south.

Slocum grinned at Buck, shaking his head in dismay. "We're going that way out."

Padre and Red Boy came back to the dry wash to join them after looking things over. Durango's camp was asleep.

Padre shook his head in the starlight. "No guards. Plenty snoring."

Slocum nodded. Was that luck or a bad sign? There wasn't any time left. "Everyone take one of them out, and then we will get the few that are left. I don't care how. Just be certain that the outlaws won't get up and fight us. These men had no mercy with the villagers. They deserve no mercy."

Padre led them all down the wash. They eased past the sleeping horses on a picket line. Slocum pointed to the pack-saddles in a pile. Everyone nodded.

Then they moved like shadows in the night. Each man went to a pallet with either gun or knife raised. They dispatched the outlaws with a clunk to the head or cut their throats.

Slocum was almost to the pallet where he figured that Durango slept.

"Stop right there, you sumbitching sawbones," Durango shouted as he sat up and raised a pistol. "You ain't cutting off my damn leg."

Three pistols shots answered him. He fell backward and dropped the gun from his grasp. One outlaw managed to get up screaming, and started to run off in the night. Bullets in his back cut him down.

"Get a couple of horses and packsaddles," Slocum ordered, reloading his Colt. "Padre, you and Red Boy watch for anyone coming from town."

Slocum went through the panniers until he found the heavy ones. Then, striking a match, he read the Spanish words on a wooden case. He looked around. Buck and Dyke were coming with the packsaddles and animals. He went over and threw more fuel on the campfire. The blaze increased the light and they strapped on the cross bucks.

Slocum staggered over under the weight and managed to boost the wooden crate in to the pannier on one side of Dyke's horse.

"Takes two to load them," he said to the others.

In minutes, four cases were loaded, and the Apaches, with their rifles ready, retreated to the fire.

"The villagers are afraid to come up here," Padre said, and shook his head as if it was nothing.

"Good," Slocum said. "Get the rest of the horses and mules. We're getting the hell out, too."

The Apaches ran off to bring them in.

In minutes, with Dyke and the Indians driving them, they were cat-hopping up a steep road for the high country.

From well up the mountainside, Slocum looked back as the first purple light of dawn made the church tower and roofs visible. It was a good thing—the outlaw and killer Durango would hurt no one ever again.

22

The music of the fandango carried above the rush of the stream and the festive voices. Slocum waltzed with the lovely widow Juanita Valdez. He still could not believe that Valdez in Mexico City had tried to storm the presidential palace with a pistol to kill the Mexican president.

What were her words? *He finally snapped.*

"You feel the money is safe in that vault?" he asked as they whirled around.

"Oh, yes, the villagers will protect it well."

"And you have money for a teacher? A better dam system for the irrigation?"

"Money for improvements. We can expand our farmland. There are many good things it can do for the people."

"Enrique would be proud. He was so worried about all of the people."

"I will see that his and Doña's deaths were not in vain."

"Good."

"Madame Mayor?" someone called out to her.

They stopped dancing, and she asked José what he wanted.

"Would you bring Slocum? They want to make a toast to all of you."

She looked at Slocum mildly. "You don't mind?"

"Who would mind going anywhere with you?"

She smiled possessively and clutched his arm. "Good. I have plans for us—later."

He looked out in the night past the silver stream. Good.

"Get Dyke and Buck over here," he said. Red Boy and Padre had already gone home with one sack of new coins each, extra horses, and new rifles.

Dyke and Buck each had lovely ladies under their arms when they joined Slocum and Señora Valdez. Slocum got up to sit on the bar. "I want to make a toast to the new mayor, Juanita Valdez."

A cheer went up and they all shouted, *"Viva Alcalde Valdez."*

"Now one for Enrique and Doña . . ."

The celebration went on and on, and ended that night for Slocum in the mayor's bed.

A week later, Slocum reined up the dun horse in the east pass. Dyke, on his white mule, and Buck, on a bay, along with two pack mules, stopped. They all looked back without many words.

"Next time some damn boy roots me out of bed when I'm with a whore to go off on some wild-goose chase," Buck said, "I'll just shoot him."

"Do that for me, too," Dyke said.

"Hell," Slocum said, shaking his head at them. "You two wouldn't have missed this for anything."

And they rode on.

Watch for

SLOCUM'S BAR-S RANCH

359th novel in the exciting SLOCUM series
from Jove

Coming in January!

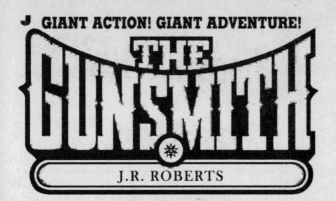

J GIANT ACTION! GIANT ADVENTURE!

THE GUNSMITH

J.R. ROBERTS

Little Sureshot And
The Wild West Show
(Gunsmith Giant #9)

Dead Weight
(Gunsmith Giant #10)

Red Mountain
(Gunsmith Giant #11)

The Knights of Misery
(Gunsmith Giant #12)

The Marshal from Paris
(Gunsmith Giant #13)

penguin.com

GIANT-SIZED ADVENTURE FROM AVENGING ANGEL LONGARM.

BY TABOR EVANS

2006 Giant Edition:

LONGARM AND THE OUTLAW EMPRESS

2007 Giant Edition:

LONGARM AND THE GOLDEN EAGLE SHOOT-OUT

2008 Giant Edition:

LONGARM AND THE VALLEY OF SKULLS